SPY HIGH:
MISSION THREE

SPY HIGH:
MISSION THREE

THE SERPENT
SCENARIO

A. J. BUTCHER

LITTLE, BROWN AND COMPANY

New York ✦ Boston

Little, Brown and Company

Time Warner Book Group
1271 Avenue of the Americas, New York, NY 10020
Visit our Web site at www.lb-teens.com

First U.S. Edition 2004
First published in Great Britain in 2003 by Atom Books

LCCN 2004101813
ISBN 0-316-73763-1 (hc) / ISBN 0-316-73766-6 (pb)

10 9 8 7 6 5 4 3 2 1

Q-FF

Printed in the United States of America

PART
ONE

CHAPTER ONE

The moon was dying.

It hung low in the night sky, as if it hardly had the strength to keep itself from falling, and it had the sickly paleness of an invalid. Its luminescence did not so much shimmer as flicker, an aging lightbulb needing replacement. Which was not so very far from the case, of course. The moon that rose above Undertown, Los Angeles, was entirely artificial.

The brainchild of a former city major, the man-made orb had originally been conceived as a crime-prevention measure. Undertown was already sinking into the gutters of lawlessness and fear. Good people were moving out; gangs were moving in. The hovering moon was intended to be a beacon of hope, a shining reminder that the rich and powerful citizens of the city Uptown had not yet forgotten their less fortunate brethren Undertown. The moon's light was supposed to drive away the darkness and keep the streets safe. Cameras were going to be fitted beneath the satellite's skin to cast a benevolent eye on all.

Only the money had run out. The mayor wasn't re-elected. Not a single lens had been installed. The moon's maintenance budget had been sliced to the bone, to the marrow of the bone.

The moon was dying, but it didn't seem to matter much. Undertown was in a much worse state.

At least, that was the way it seemed to the girl. The streets that she'd known so well, the sidewalks that had tumbled and teemed with life once upon a time, when she'd been small and smiling, were now dark and cold and empty. All right, it was late, past midnight, but the girl could sense dereliction in the air, and decay, and despair, like food left to rot.

And in this tomb of silence, she sensed footsteps behind her, footsteps following her. Three pairs, trying to be stealthy but heavy on the sidewalk. Males. Pursuers.

The girl narrowed her brilliant emerald eyes. She doubted they wanted to ask her directions.

As if afraid to view what might happen next, the moon dimmed, yellowed with jaundice.

The girl heard the footsteps increase their pace. She didn't look back. She'd see their faces soon enough.

Briefly, the moon rallied, blooming a sudden, perfect white. Then there was a rattle, an electronic sigh, and the power failed. The moon was blown out like a candle. It was truly night.

The girl stopped. Her pursuers didn't.

"Hey, girlie!"

The girl put down her bag. She felt she might need both hands free for this.

"Are you talking to me?" She saw them now as they caught up with her, swaggered around her, admired her lithe figure and the sweep of hair as dark as night. A United Nations of muggers: one black; one white, beneath the eruptions of acne; and one Chinese like herself. He was the biggest.

"What are you doing out here all alone . . . ?"

". . . Yeah it's late and you look like you should be tucked in your bed."

"Don't you know these streets are dangerous?"

"Is that so? Thanks for telling me. I'll bear it in mind."

"So how's about showing some gratitude, then?" They shuffled into position, in front, behind, to the right, cutting off any escape route. To her left was the wall.

"Your bag, girlie. We want your bag." The tone was threatening now. Their muscles tensing.

"Well," said the girl, "you'd better come and get it, then."

She took the Chinese guy down before he could even flinch — a lightning karate chop. The black guy behind, she'd expertly judged his height, and directed her kick accordingly. The white guy, eyes wide, went for a knife. The girl went for him. Twisted, yanked. Even a knife wouldn't help with a dislocated arm.

With her would-be assailants groaning on the ground, the girl assumed a defensive posture. Though she also assumed she wouldn't need it. She was right.

"Who are you, girlie?" The muggers groped to their feet, kept their distance. "You shouldn't be here, the likes of you." They staggered back down the street, broke into a shambling run. "You don't belong here. You don't belong!" Their final call, and more painful to the girl than anything they could have done physically.

Because she *did* belong here. Right here.

As the moon clicked into life again, like a happy ending, the girl gazed up at the apartment building alongside her and her green cat eyes filled with tears. She did belong here.

Jennifer Chen had come home.

Lesson Thirteen was *In the Restaurant*. A very nice restaurant it was, too, al fresco dining under a brightly striped canopy with attractive views of the cobbled street and opposite the ornate baroque buildings. The charming and attentive waitstaff in black vests and bow ties whisked silver trays piled high with food and ice buckets boasting vintage bottles of champagne to the delighted clientele. Location? Eddie's best guess was maybe somewhere in the Balkans.

"So Cally," he said, "what's Serbo-Croat for pastrami on rye and plenty of ketchup with my fries, please?" He scratched his untidy red hair quizzically.

"Oh, Eddie. Just say it," sighed Cally Cross. "You know your Babel chip will translate whatever you say into the appropriate language. And the same with what the waiters say to us. Honestly, Ed. I think when they implanted the chip, they took out your brain."

"Never found a brain, did they, Eddie?" said Lori Angel. "But never mind. We like you just the way you are. Now, what shall I order?" She swept her long blond hair back and focused her sparkling blue eyes on the menu.

"Lori," complained Ben Stanton, "the eating isn't important. It's the espionage that matters. We were supposed to meet our contact here —" Ben glanced at the clock with Roman numerals set high into the wall of the house opposite, above an open window — "and he's already late."

"Sexist assumption, Ben," Eddie pointed out. "Our contact could be a she."

"Who cares?" grumbled Jake Daly, slumping back in his chair. "And who cares if he or she isn't quite as obsessed with punctuality as you are, leader man?"

"I care," Ben declared angrily. "You should care. We all should. Death is in the details, how many times have we been told that?"

"You're right, Ben," soothed Lori. "We need to be alert. Jake knows that." Her eyes sought to persuade him to apologize but Jake, arms crossed defensively, seemed oblivious to concession. She knew what was really upsetting him. Five people sat around the table when there should have been six.

Ben returned his own gaze more thoughtfully to the clock. "That window," he considered, "why is it open?"

"I doubt they've heard of air-conditioning in these parts, Ben," said Cally. "From the way they're looking at me, they can't have heard of African-Americans, either. Or maybe it's just my dreads." She shook her beaded dreadlocks for emphasis.

"No, it's the only open window on the whole side of that street." The others saw that Ben was right. "And by coincidence, it's exactly across from us." He frowned. "Something's wrong."

"You can say that again," Eddie observed as several waiters approached, all carrying covered trays. "We haven't even ordered yet, and they're bringing us food. What's Serbo-Croat for sorry, you've got the wrong table?"

"I've got a sinking feeling they haven't," Ben tensed, words of warning in his mouth.

He didn't have time to utter them. At that point the waiters most unprofessionally dropped their trays. Not that it bothered them, because they weren't waiters at all. Their true profession was far deadlier, and the covered trays had concealed not food but weapons.

They shot Eddie first, the impact knocking both him and his chair backward, almost comically. Jake and Cally dived for cover beneath the table. Ben and Lori took more offensive action, wielding their chairs as shields then as bludgeons. Jake and Cally tried to follow suit with the table, upending it and using it to ram their attackers. Good idea in principle, but it left their backs exposed. Laser bolts pulsed into Cally. Jake turned, stared down the barrel of a shock gun. "Jake, move!" He didn't. The waiter shot him.

"Lori, let's get out of here. Now!" Ben hurled his chair at two of the assassins. A third was struggling with Lori, one hand fending off her chair, the other trying to aim a sawed-off pulse gun. Ben seized a discarded tray, flung it like a Frisbee. It nearly took the waiter's head off.

Lori turned toward Ben. She was smiling. There was the crack of a shot from across the street. And then she wasn't.

"Lori!" Ben's eyes flashed to the open window. Now he knew why it had looked odd — snipers couldn't work through glass. For once, it gave Ben no pleasure to be proved right. Not that the feeling would have lasted long, anyway. He saw a second flash from the window and knew what was coming faster than the sound it made.

Lights out.

"Lights on," said Senior Tutor Elmore Grant. He regarded a shamefaced Bond Team as they hunched disconsolately in his study. "It doesn't get any prettier with repeated viewings, does it? Anybody have anything to say?"

"If those waiter guys are expecting a tip, they can forget it."

"Anything worth saying, Eddie." Apparently not. "Because I can't believe that the team whose abject failure on the Spyscape I've just witnessed is the same group of individuals who won the Sherlock Shied only a week ago."

"We're not the same, sir," said Jake bitterly. "We're missing Jennifer." He sat hunched up like a spring, his powerful body tensed, dark eyes glowering from beneath the tangled mop of his black hair.

"Of course. Of course." Grant sighed and ran his hands through his hair. What he'd expected. "I'm well aware of Jennifer's —" he picked his words carefully — "absence. But you're letting it affect your performance, and in our line of work, you can't allow that to happen."

"Jennifer's our teammate, sir," objected Jake while the others winced, Ben in particular. "More than that. She's our friend." *And even more than that to me*, he thought, *or might have been*. "How are we supposed to just forget her? How can you forget someone you care about?"

"Discipline, Jake," said Grant firmly, though not entirely unsympathetically. "Focus. Training. You do it because if you intend to continue here at Deveraux Academy, you have to learn to put your personal feelings aside, whatever they are, for the good of the cause. None of us is more important than the mission. To be a successful secret agent, you have to be single-minded."

"I think, sir," Lori felt she ought to speak in Jake's defense, "what Jake means is that it's the uncertainty that's getting us down. We don't know why Jennifer left as suddenly as she did, we don't know where she's gone, and we don't know what's going to happen to her when she's found or to us in the meantime."

"Lori's right, sir," agreed Cally. "Are we going to get a new member, or is Jennifer going to be allowed back?"

"She can't be allowed back, can she, sir?" Ben asked, earning a resentful glare from Jake. "Leaving the school without permission, I mean, just running off, I thought the rules were clear on that: mind-wipe and expulsion."

Lori saw Jake's fists clench. Ben was correct, but she wished he hadn't sounded so eager. And she wished that Jennifer hadn't forced this situation to arise.

"Technically, the rules are clear," allowed Grant. "Mind-wipe and expulsion. But the thing about rules, Ben, even the regulations at Spy High, is that there are always possible exceptions. Now I'm not saying that Jennifer's case is one. I'm not really in a position to tell you anything more than what you already know. Mr. Deveraux has been appraised of the situation and will decide what is to be done in due course."

"But . . ." Jake wasn't satisfied.

"It's out of your hands, Bond Team. It's out of mine." Grant shook his head regretfully. "That Jennifer's actions will have consequences is certain, but one of them must not be to distract you from your studies. Any more disasters like today, and Mr. Deveraux might start to wonder whether there aren't five further candidates for mind-wiping. Think about it."

Bond Team didn't need to be told. It weighed on their minds like lead as they trudged to the girls' room and shut themselves away inside. Nobody sat on Jennifer's bed. Nobody even went close. It remained untouched, unused, like a shrine.

But Jake stared at it. Apart from the removal of the sheets, nobody had touched anything of Jennifer's in the week since her disappearance, and yet something was missing, Jake sensed, something important. If he could think what it was, he'd know what to do. Stanton was pacing up and down, moaning drearily about their prospects to anyone who'd listen. Jake didn't. Stanton had never liked Jennifer, not really. He'd tolerated her because they were in the same team, but he'd also condescended toward her in his usual arrogant blond-haired and blue-eyed

rich-kid-of-the-month way. Jennifer had always been too vola-
tile for Ben to handle, too much her own person. But then, had
he, Jake, understood her any better? If he had, how come she'd
pulled the biggest vanishing trick of all time without even saying good-bye?

All she'd left was a note. Not addressed to him but addressed to Cally and Lori. He'd memorized every word.

*Dear Cally and Lori, I'm sorry I've had to leave like this, but one day
perhaps you'll understand. There's something I have to do. Something I've always known I'd have to do, and now it's time. Don't think too badly of me.
They'll find someone else to fill my place. I'm not important. Say good-bye to
the others for me. Say good-bye to Jake. Tell him I'm sorry. Tell him to forget
all about me and to look ahead. You've all got a future. I've only ever had a
past. Good luck. Jen.*

Jennifer's past. A past she'd kept buried, as a body in a coffin. Jake knew nothing about her life before Spy High, except
what her brother and parents looked like, preserved in that photograph she always kept on her bedside table.

The photograph that was gone. *That* was what was missing.
Suddenly, Jake understood.

"And what about you, Daly?" Ben was still criticizing. "You
just stood there, inviting the assassin to pick his target, like you
couldn't be bothered."

"I couldn't be bothered. Go sell noticed," said Jake. "I've got
more important things on my mind than playing a spy. Like
finding Jennifer. And I think I know where we need to look."
The others turned to Jake. "She took the photo of her family
with her. With what she said in the letter about the past, it can
mean only one thing — she's gone home, wherever that is. Jennifer's gone home."

"Even if you're right, Jake, that's not much help," Lori pointed out. "None of us know where Jen's home is."

"But we can find out. We can access her personal file."

"Oh, no," Ben spluttered. "Don't even go there, Daly. Student files are confidential. Access is strictly forbidden to anyone but Deveraux and Grant. It's in the rules."

Jake grinned conspiratorially. "And what did Grant just say? About there always being possible exceptions? Who votes we make this one?"

The hallways seemed narrower than before. They were certainly darker, but Jennifer had never been afraid of the dark. There didn't appear to be any power in the building, though perhaps she shouldn't be surprised. There didn't appear to be any tenants, either. All gone. All left. Maybe all dead. There were ugly words scarring the walls.

She climbed the stairs to the first floor, slowly, carefully. She'd sat on these stairs once and chattered with Kim. They'd played with their dolls and decided who they'd marry when they were big girls. Nobody would want to sit on these stairs now. The filth of dereliction was everywhere.

At the landing, Jennifer turned left. Past the apartment where old Mrs. Koerner used to live, with her ancient radio and even more ancient car. Past the apartment where the young couple could have been heard making strange noises at odd times of the afternoon and Mom always said, "Shocking. Some people have no shame." The noises would certainly be audible now. The apartment no longer had a door.

And then, at the end of the corridor, Apartment Twenty. Home. *"Yes, I know it's a big number, Jennifer, but you'll be able to remember it because if you count all your fingers and all your toes, that's the same number."* The door was still on its hinges, though the lock was splintered. Thieves, maybe. Or squatters. She could enter if she wanted to. No need to knock. It had always been a good part of the day when they'd heard Daddy's key in the lock, and it meant he was home after work, and she and her little brother, Shang, would run to greet him, and he'd lift them up so effortlessly because he was so strong then, so alive. . . .

But that was then, not now.

Jennifer steeled herself, the emotions of the past flooding through her, threatening to drown her. She pressed her trembling hand against the door. And pushed.

"I'm in!" Cally exulted.

"Quietly, Cal," urged Jake. "We don't want any interruptions."

"No, I expect *you* don't," snorted Ben, stressing the second person. He'd already emphasized his displeasure at what his teammates were doing by standing aloof and apart from them as they crammed around the computer screen. He scarcely believed that even Cally would hack her way into Spy High's systems without alerting somebody to the intrusion, and when security charged into the computer room, mind-wipers at the ready, Benjamin T. Stanton Jr. did not want to be implicated with the rest. He wasn't going to allow his future to be jeopardized by the aberrations of Jennifer Chen. It kind of shocked him that the others didn't seem to worry.

Especially Lori. Lori was his girl. He thought he could expect support from her. Instead, she turned to him now: "Come and look, Ben. See what we've found."

"Any swimsuit photos or anything like that?" said Eddie, leering.

"Jennifer's address. Everything."

"Everything's right." Cally's voice thickened. "No wonder she kept quiet about her past."

"Oh my God," breathed Jake.

"Jennifer's family," Cally said in a funeral voice. "They're dead."

Ben surprised himself more than the others. "How?"

Cally read the details in a tone hollow with hurt. "They were murdered, Jennifer's parents, her little brother — by members of some street gang called the Serpents. It says Jen's dad refused to pay for protection. So the Serpents murdered them. Right in front of Jennifer's eyes. My God, she was eight years old, and she saw it all. They left her alive as an example to others. They left her in her apartment with the bodies of her parents and her brother around her." She looked at her teammates, eyes reddened like they'd been bleeding. "Nobody was ever found for the murders. Nobody was ever charged."

There were ghosts in the apartment. Even though the rooms were bare and barren, Jennifer could see them through the darkness as they'd once been, the furniture was in place, and the people. The television over there by the window, the television that her dad was always going to trade in for one of those new videoscreen models but never did. Jennifer saw it, heard the program, a sitcom set in the lunar colony, heard the laughter that wasn't real. She saw her mom and dad again, in their armchairs, and she wanted to run to them and hug them, and little Shang playing on the carpet, making sounds of war.

The ghosts of her family. The ghosts of that night.

Then the doorbell rang. The doorbell that no longer existed.

"I'll go," Dad said. Had said.

"No," Jennifer sobbed, reaching out across the years with futile fingers. "Daddy, don't. Don't go. It's him. It's him at the door."

There were shouts. Cries. Anger. And Jennifer's dad was forced back into the room by a gang of grinning thugs, one of them with holes instead of eyes, or they could have been dark glasses. And at their heart, their stinking, twisted heart, was the serpent-man, the man in the skin of a snake.

He was looking over Jennifer now as he'd done then, and his knife was red now as it had been then, and she could see that his scales were tattoos. There were tattoos all over his body.

"*No!*" Jennifer swept the ghosts away, fought for control. She closed her eyes and when she opened them, the apartment was an empty shell again, silent, abandoned, and desolate.

Aunt Li's apartment was on the edge of Undertown, the proceeds from Uncle Fung's life insurance policy allowing his widow a tantalizing glimpse of a more respectable neighborhood. When she opened the door to Jennifer, she gasped first and then burst into tears. Recovering quickly, however, as Aunt Li always did from life's twists and turns, she went on to do something altogether more useful. She made breakfast.

"You shouldn't have been too surprised to see me, Aunt Li," Jennifer said from the table as her aunt cooked eggs, bacon, and pancakes and brewed hot coffee. "You wrote to me in the first place, telling me . . ." She paused, rephrased her original sentence, eyes dark like death, ". . . telling me the news. You must have known I'd come."

"Not at six-thirty in the morning, love," said Aunt Li. "Will you be staying here? There's not much room, but you're quite welcome. . . ."

"No. Thanks." Jennifer was firm. "I'll be staying at home for as long as this takes. That's where I spent the night, why I'm here so early."

"I see." Aunt Li considered carefully. "Is that wise?"

"It's how I want it."

The woman nodded acceptantly and served her niece breakfast.

Jennifer grasped her wrist, more tightly than she'd probably intended. "And you're sure it's him, Aunt Li? You've seen him?"

"I haven't, darling, no, but others have. It's him. The tattoos like the scales of a snake. There's no mistake, I'm afraid."

"Don't be afraid. Be glad. Soon Mom, Dad, and Shang will be able to rest in peace."

"But wouldn't it be simpler, safer, to inform the police, Jennifer? You never even gave them a description. They might have been able to find this man years ago."

"Yeah." Jennifer's eyes blazed with bitterness. "And locked him away for a bit. And then let him out. No, Aunt Li, that would never have been good enough, not what I want at all."

"What do you want, Jennifer?" said Aunt Li.

"Isn't it obvious?" Jennifer began eating her breakfast. "I want to kill him."

CHAPTER TWO

While Spy High was different to most other schools in almost every way, it was still customary in the small hours of the morning for its students to be in their beds and sound asleep. It was not usual for five of them to be congregated in one room together and certainly not for anybody to be packing as if for immediate departure. Which was what Jake seemed to be doing.

"At the risk of repeating myself one final time," Ben said, "this is a very dumb idea."

"At the risk of repeating myself also," replied Jake, "you don't really want to know how little I care, do you, Ben?"

"Stop squabbling, you two," scolded Cally. "We're supposed to be a team, remember?"

"There was a time when we acted like it," Ben said. "Now everybody's running off to pursue their own agendas."

Jake threw a final item of clothing into his case as if he'd prefer to be aiming at Ben's head. "Listen, Stanton, what else is there to do? We've got a good idea where Jennifer's gone, half a good idea as to why, and we can't just leave her to it. Doing nothing is not an option."

"We could tell Grant." But even Ben felt that was a lame, somehow sneaky thing to say or do. "Or I guess not," he corrected himself.

"Jen's a member of Bond Team," said Lori. "Bond Team looks after its own."

"You can look after me any day, Lo," teased Eddie. "Hey, and Jakey, don't forget your deodorant. It's hot on the coast."

"Leaving the rest of us to face the flak." Ben wasn't finished yet. "Maybe disciplinary procedures."

"That's typical of you, Stanton," scoffed Jake. "Not bothered about Jennifer at all, just what might happen to you, a blot on the perfect record."

"Jake," Lori snapped. "That's not fair."

Jake relented a little. Maybe he had gone too far. He just wanted to be away, after Jennifer. Whatever was going to happen was going to happen. "All right. Okay. Uncalled for. But Ben, if it was Lori missing, Lori maybe in trouble, wouldn't you be the first to do what I'm doing now?"

Ben hung his head. He didn't feel it was a reasonable question to be asked with Lori present. "If you put it like that," he felt obliged to say. "You go, Jake. We'll cover for you. Like Lori said, Bond Team looks after its own."

"Another moving Kleenex moment," said Eddie.

Lori accompanied Jake to one of the school's side doors. It hadn't been thought wise for them all to traipse through the corridor at three in the morning.

"This is it, then," Jake said softly. "Cab should be waiting outside the grounds. Cally's hacked me onto a flight to LA. I'll call you when I find Jennifer."

"Make sure you do, Jake," Lori returned. Because they were both whispering, they were very close together. She could feel his breath on her cheek. "I hope you find what else you're looking for, too. With Jennifer. You deserve to be happy."

"You think so?"

"All that help you gave me with Simon Macey? I know so. Good luck, Jake."

"Thanks, Lori." And they hugged. For quite a long time.

When she finally turned away from watching Jake become invisible in the darkness, Lori found that her eyes were filled with tears.

Someone had once said that high school were the best days of your life. Whoever it was had obviously never been to school in Undertown, Los Angeles. The crumbling heaps of bricks and mortar with Jennifer Chen waiting outside seemed more like the remains of a war zone than an educational institution. Students slunk between them like terrorists; she half expected to see the teachers wearing bulletproof vests. If you were looking for a stimulating learning experience, it seemed you'd better look elsewhere, maybe toward the glittering, lofty towers of Uptown that could be glimpsed faintly and far off, like an unobtainable dream, like a hope for the future that could never come true. Jennifer set her lips grimly. If a selector from Deveraux hadn't seen her and spotted her potential, if Senior Tutor Grant hadn't approached her with the offer of a place at Spy High, she'd probably be attending this very school, her life chances as dilapidated as its buildings.

But she'd taken her place. She'd trained at Spy High. And now she was going to use that training for the purpose she'd always intended: revenge on the man who'd killed her family.

She wondered if she'd recognize Kim when the school day ended and the students left. It had been awhile. They'd promised to always keep in touch. To be best friends, *"Best friends forever."* But after the murders, Jennifer had moved away to live with Aunt Li and Uncle Fung. Then she'd moved further away from Kim to the East Coast and the Deveraux Academy. Distances that, perhaps, were not only literal.

In Jennifer's mind, she could see two little Chinese girls in identical clothes, with identical smiles, holding hands and skipping in the street. "You sure you aren't sisters, you two?" old Mrs. Koerner had said, her sight dim behind her glasses, as the young Kim and Jennifer giggled. "You're more like sisters."

Kim might look slightly different now — as she did herself — but nothing could eradicate the past. Jennifer needed help, and she trusted Kim to supply it.

The school bell screamed like an air-raid siren. Students scattered, rushing past Jennifer as if they expected bombs to start falling any second. Jennifer stood her ground and watched. Kim had been nine years old the last time they'd talked. Five years of change. She doubted there'd be pigtails now, or little white socks, or a doll hanging from her hand.

She was right. There were none of those things. Kim Tang wore the typically loose, shapeless garments of a teenager, her ink-black hair that had once been longer than Jennifer's own was now cropped short like some kind of penance, and she held not a toy in her hand but a cigarette, which she smoked with the automatic regularity born of much practice.

A pang of nostalgia squeezed Jennifer's heart.

"Kim!" she called out. "Kim!"

Her old friend heard. For a moment her expression seemed fearful, hunted. Then she saw Jennifer running toward her and for another moment there was blankness. But maybe a moment after five years wasn't bad. Next would come the "Great to see you."

"Jennifer? What are you doing in a hole like this?"

* * *

"If we keep on like this, maybe they'll give us a season ticket," Eddie had said. Being summoned to Grant's study did seem to be becoming a habit for Bond Team. Each time there was a little more room for them to fit in. Because each time there seemed to be fewer members of Bond Team.

They'd tried to keep Jake's absence undetected for as long as possible. They'd told Ms. Bannon at Weapons Instruction that they hadn't seen Jake that morning, but he was probably in the infirmary because he hadn't been feeling too well last night, he'd said so. Ms. Bannon had shrugged and turned her attention back to laser-guided pulse rifles. They'd told Senior Tutor Grant the same story in History of Espionage. Grant, however, perhaps demonstrating why he was senior tutor, immediately contacted the infirmary and learned that not only was Jake Daly not languishing in a bed there now, but had not felt the need to consult a member of the medical staff since before Christmas, and then only because of a slightly sprained ankle.

Hence the meeting in Grant's study.

It was worse than before, Ben knew that. This time, Jonathan Deveraux himself was directly involved, the screen on the tutor's desk displaying his grave and finely sculpted features. As usual, there was no personal appearance from the college's founder, and Ben sought to take heart from that. Surely, if this was going to be an expulsion matter, even the notoriously reclusive Mr. Deveraux, whom no student had ever seen in the flesh, would physically be there to take charge? On the other hand, though, the founder's cool and clinical gaze upon them was worrying enough.

"So," said Deveraux, in a tone pitched midway between

accusation and amusement, "to misplace one team member is unfortunate but to misplace two seems like carelessness."

"It's my fault, sir, my responsibility." Ben raised his impressively square chin and tried to look noble. The trouble with being team leader, he thought, was that now and again he had to act like one. "I should have known Jake might do something like this."

"Something like what, Stanton?" Deveraux's diamond-chipped eyes narrowed.

"Well, he's gone after Jennifer, hasn't he?" Was the founder testing him? Surely they'd assumed that much. "I mean, that's what we . . . why else would he just up and leave?"

"You may very well be right, Stanton," said Deveraux, "but Daly gave you no indication that he was planning to depart, for whatever reason?"

"No, sir," Ben lied, guilt forcing his eyes downward.

"Not to any of us, sir," Lori supported.

"Absolutely not." Cally, too.

"He never talks to me about anything." Eddie made the ignorance unanimous.

"Such great loyalty to his teammates," observed Deveraux, "if Daly has indeed risked his future at Spy High in order to pursue Jennifer Chen as you all believe. A loyalty that I can see extends throughout Bond Team."

Was that sarcasm? Ben feared. Did Deveraux realize that they weren't telling the truth? What did he know?

"Is there anything else you'd like to tell us?"

Oh, yeah, Ben thought. *We also hacked into the college's confidential personal files, and did you know that Jen's family was slaughtered by a street gang?* "No, sir," he said. "Nothing."

"Then this meeting is terminated," Deveraux said.

"Sir?" Lori. "About Jake, sir, and Jennifer, too, I suppose. What's going to happen now?"

The wryest of smiles played around the founder's lips. "Now," he said, "only time will tell."

"He knows," Ben groaned, throwing himself back on his bed. "Deveraux knows everything. He's bound to. We're dead."

"You think?" Eddie shook his head mournfully. "And I had such a great future."

"Don't be too sure," Cally cautioned.

"What? About my future?"

"Eddie, why don't you suddenly adopt meditation as a hobby, like immediately? I mean about Deveraux. He might have his suspicions, but he can't be certain. Neither can Grant. I covered our tracks pretty well on the system. Nobody'll even know we've been in."

"You hope," Ben said gloomily.

"I was proud of you back there, Ben." Lori tried to lighten the mood. "Taking the blame on yourself like that. If Jake knew, I'm sure he'd appreciate it."

She failed.

"Oh, great. Excellent." Ben laughed at the absurdity of it all. "So we all of us talk our way into a mind-wipe, and you're 'sure' that Jake will 'appreciate it.' Well, that makes me fell a lot better, Lori. Hope it does the same for you." Jake and even Jennifer had never exactly been Ben's favorite members of Bond Team. He was struggling not to feel aggrieved by the situation their actions seemed to have forced him into. "I hope it keeps you warm at night. Because after we're expelled, when we wake up one morning and can't remember one another or even having met or been here at Spy High at all, let's hope that a little bit of Jake's appreciation'll make the sacrifice worthwhile. Me, though, I have my doubts."

There hadn't been hugs, but that was okay. It didn't mean anything. Kim probably felt a little too self-conscious to express her feelings physically in front of new friends who'd never seen Jennifer before. Kim hadn't seen her in years. She was bound to be surprised.

"You've come back, Jen." Staggered would be more like it. Incredulous. As if Jennifer had done a Lazarus and risen from the dead. "Why?"

"We need to talk, Kim. I'll explain everything. But hey, it's good to see you again."

They went to Gaudini's, of course, just the two of them. There'd been a time when the coffee bar had seemed the epitome of glitz and glamour to the two girls from Undertown, when the golden letters of its name, inscribed so dashingly across its glittering windows, had suggested both drama and romance, where discreet tables and quiet corners had promised secret encounters with a grown-up world that neither Jennifer nor Kim had yet experienced. Now the name was peeling and faded, the interior poky, dusty, like a wonderful present left too long and forgotten. Mr. Gaudini himself looked too old still to be working, and the coffee he served them came in chipped cups and had slopped into the saucers.

Jennifer sighed. Another illusion shattered. But at least she could still rely on Kim. "Where do you want to sit?"

"Gee, I don't know. We might have a wait," said Kim sarcastically. The girls were Gaudini's only customers.

"Place has seen better days," Jennifer observed as they chose a corner table.

"Hasn't everywhere?" retorted Kim. "Hasn't everyone?"

"What are you talking about? Looking good, Kim."

"Need laser treatment on the eyes, Jen. I'm looking like crap. My mirror lets me know every morning. You remember how old Mrs. Koerner never used to be able to tell us apart?" For a second the ghost of a smile fluttered at Kim's lips. She gazed at Jennifer's glossy tide of hair, her perfect oval face. "Don't reckon she'd have the same problem now, do you? Mind if I smoke?" Jennifer didn't. "Want one?" Didn't again. "You still at that posh school I heard you went to? What was it? Dev something?"

"Deveraux. The Deveraux Academy."

"Hum. Bet there's no smoking at the Deveraux Academy, right?" Kim took a deep drag of her cigarette, like she half wanted to choke herself. "Why aren't you there now? Holiday or something?"

"Not quite."

"Not got expelled, have you?"

"Not yet." Jennifer smiled mysteriously.

"Little bit of a rebel still, are you?" Kim nodded in approval. "So why *are* you here, Jen? It is kind of nostalgic to see you, girlfriend, don't get me wrong, but why now? I've got a feeling it's not just for old time's sake."

"Oh, it is, Kim." Jennifer's expression darkened. "Just not the old times you mean."

Kim understood. "Your parents."

"And Shang. Don't forget my baby brother. He'd be eleven next month if, well, you know. *If.*"

"Look, Jen, I can't begin to understand how you must have felt when it happened, how you must feel now, but coming back to Undertown, I don't see how that's going to help. You should be letting the scars heal, not tearing open old wounds."

Jennifer leaned forward eagerly, intensely. "I've got information," she said, "about the man who did it."

Now it was Kim's expression that darkened. Identical, like they'd been as children. "Don't go there, Jen," she warned. "Don't even think of going there. Whatever you think you know, forget it. You can't change the past, no one can, and it sounds like you've got some sort of future to look forward to at this academy place, which is more than those of us have. Don't risk throwing that away by getting in over your head back here. Listen, Jen, you want my advice?"

"I want your help, Kim."

"My advice is leave now and don't look back. You don't belong here anymore, Jen. You don't know what it's like."

Jennifer opened her mouth, but whether to protest or agree, Kim never found out. At that moment the great glass window of Gaudini's exploded inward, spraying the restaurant with jagged shards like shavings of ice. Kim screamed, threw herself against the back wall. Jennifer also jumped to her feet, but only to assume a defensive stance. Her Spy High training worked just as well in Undertown as anywhere else.

And she might be needing it. Two youths, barely out of their teens, leaped through the gaping hole in the window, male and female, maybe a couple. They certainly seemed to have a lot in common. Black clothes. White skin. White like frost or death or the flag of surrender. Blood-red eyes. Blood-red lips. Hands like claws. And teeth. Jennifer registered them as thin lips peeled back in a chilling parody of a smile. Teeth like the cutting edge of a hacksaw. The intruders recognized fear in Gaudini's. They enjoyed it. They seemed to want to add to it.

"Jen, watch out!"

Jennifer didn't really need Kim's warning, though she appreciated the sentiment. The male youth was rushing directly at her, his movement jerky, convulsive, as though some kind of current was coursing through him. He was quick but clumsy. A hopeless attack. Jennifer smacked her fist into his torso, shuddered at the impact. Her assailant halted in mid-charge. Dazed, he might have collapsed, anyway. Jennifer's second blow helped him on his way.

"Wow, Jennifer!" gaped Kim, and then: "Gaudini!"

But Mr. Gaudini evidently did not require assistance in dealing with the second youth. From under the counter, he whipped an old pump-action stasis rifle, fired it point-blank at the girl like he knew what he was doing. She cried out, juddered as the paralysis took swift effect, fell to the floor stiffly. And didn't get up.

"You kids all right?" said Mr. Gaudini.

"Yeah, thanks. We're fine." Jennifer was already kneeling by the unconscious form of her attacker, inspecting him more closely.

"Okay. I'm calling the cops."

"Where did you learn moves like that?" Kim admired. "You took the Drac out without even blinking."

"What did you call him?" Jennifer avoided touching the pallid flesh again, but the youth's unconscious form filled her with an uncomfortable fascination.

"He's a Drac addict. They both are. The skin. The teeth. Like fangs. We were lucky. Drac's the foulest habit of them all."

"What do you mean?"

"It's a new drug," Kim supplied. "Hasn't been on the streets long, but it's already making its mark. They say it gives you the greatest rush you can imagine, makes you feel like you're a god, immortal, all-powerful, like there's nothing you can't do, nothing you can't be. Trouble is, the high comes with a low, and the low's not good. You get addicted to Drac, and you've signed up for your coffin. It changes you, see? Turns you into that." She gestured at the pale body with disgust. "And there's no way back. These guys weren't muggers after our money, Jen. They were after our blood, and I mean literally."

Jennifer looked up, horrified.

"It's like I said, Jen," Kim urged. "You don't know what's been happening around here. Just leave now and don't look back."

"Leave now," her oldest friend had said. But how could she do that? *"Don't look back."* How could she not? The blood of her family was on her conscience. It had to be avenged.

Under the glittering moon, through sordid, silent streets Jennifer picked her way home. Only it wasn't home now at all; it hadn't been since That Night. Their apartment had been left empty. Understandably, nobody really wanted to live and sleep in rooms where murder had been committed. The whole place seemed blighted, stained. People had moved away, even the

Tangs, even old Mrs. Koerner. And nobody had moved in, not even squatters.

As Jennifer wearily entered her apartment, she knew that, but for her, the building was deserted.

Only it wasn't.

Jennifer tensed among liquid shadows. Someone was there. Hearing sharpened by Spy High's aural enhancement program detected soft breathing, quiet movement. She wanted to scream but didn't.

From out of the darkness, a hand reached toward her.

CHAPTER THREE

Jennifer reacted instinctively, seized the hand and pulled, turned her body to throw the intruder, and sent him crashing to the floor. In her mind, she was sure it was him — the tattooed man. It could only be him.

There was a cry of pain as he slammed onto bare boards. "Okay, okay. It's good to see you, too, though I'm not sure my ribs would agree."

"Jake." She seemed amazed, astounded. "Jake?" The familiar dark features, the tangle of hair.

"We thought you might need some help."

She lit a feeble lamp and made coffee which they drank sitting on an old piece of matting that she'd scrounged from Aunt Li. For a long time, they didn't talk.

"How did you find me?" The obvious first question, tentatively phrased.

"Cally hacked into the computer. We read your file."

In the semidarkness, Jennifer didn't need to look away to avoid Jake's gaze, but she did anyway, out of the lamplight, blackness draining her face. "So you know," she said. "About my family."

"Yes. I can't imagine . . . I'm so sorry."

"Came a long way to express your sympathies. Could have sent a card."

"That's not why I'm here, Jen."

An unnecessary laugh, a strange sound in the shrouded apartment. "How is everything back at Spy High, anyway?

Seems a world away, a lifetime. Is Grant on the warpath? What about Ben? I doubt I'm flavor of the month with him right now."

"It doesn't matter."

"Well, when you leave, Jake, you can take my apologies with you. I wish I'd had time to say good-bye properly, but things never seem to work out like you'd wish."

"That's for sure," said Jake. "Because I'm not leaving, Jen."

"What?" Her voice almost breaking. "But you've got to. This is my business, Jake. It has nothing to do with you."

"What hasn't?" Jake leaned forward earnestly. "Why are you even here, Jennifer?"

"I can't tell you. It's not . . ."

"It has to do with your parents, doesn't it? We've worked out that much."

"I said it's not your problem."

"Tell me. Jen, you've got to tell me. I'm here for you. I want to help." And hold her. And comfort her. He wanted all that, too. "You've got to let me in."

"I can't!" Jennifer was on her feet, agonizing, struggling with herself. "Because the man who murdered my parents is back, and it's my responsibility to make him pay, not anybody else's but mine. I have to do it for my parents' sake." She paused, looked pleadingly toward Jake. "Or what would my life have been for?"

"Jen . . ."

"So this isn't a world-conquering maniac I'm dealing with. This isn't a Stromfeld or a Frankenstein or a Nemesis. It's no business of Spy High. So you can leave now, Jake, go back to saving the universe. Forget about the little people. Forget about me."

"Is that what you really want?" Somehow, they'd drifted together. Somehow, they were almost touching. "Tell it to my face, Jen. Look me in the eye, and tell me you want me to go. Do it now."

His eyes burned with feeling. "I want . . ."

She stared into the darkness. She'd been alone with her pain and her tragedy for so long, and she suddenly couldn't handle it anymore. Not now. She needed him. "Stay, Jake." The words were molten, torn from somewhere deep. "I want you to stay."

"So far, your History of Espionage course has been exactly that," said Senior Tutor Elmore Grant, "a study of the past, but there is an element to it that we have yet to explore." Bond Team, or at least its four remaining members, slumped listlessly in the classroom, doing a most convincing job of pretending not to be interested. "It has been said that those who fail to learn the lessons of history —"

"Are put in detention for the rest of their natural life," muttered Eddie.

"— are doomed to repeat them," finished Grant. "This is not an error we intend to commit at Deveraux Academy. We look to the past to see how it has shaped the present. We look at the present to anticipate how it might shape the future. It's called Threat Analysis, and we have people who spend their entire careers working on it, identifying trends and events of possible concern in the hope of preventing them from becoming fully fledged problems later on. Consider this, for example."

The classroom was subjected to a sudden barrage of sights and sounds. Three-dimensional snippets of news film bulged between the students — a political rally marching over Eddie's head, Cally launched into space with the new Sun Probe, Ben among the crowd at the World Cup Final, Lori languishing with a bawling child in a Middle Eastern refugee camp. And there were voices, too, in the languages of five continents, fluttering about their ears like birds, raised in sorrow, raised in joy, shouting, soothing, reasoned, ranting, callous, emotional, personal, political. A single second of the world's activity crammed into the classroom, overwhelming and incomprehensible.

And gone as abruptly as it had appeared.

"Put that in an alarm clock, and you'd make a fortune," Eddie said.

"Difficult to make sense of it all, hmm?" Grant smiled. "But that's what our Intelligence Gathering Center is for. The IGC doesn't simply record what's going on in the world today, and every day, but it assists our Threat Analysis experts in singling out those moments that could be of significance for tomorrow."

"But, sir," Lori raised her hand, "everything's significant to somebody, isn't it?"

"Indeed," acknowledged Grant, "but remember, Lori, in espionage, as I hope this course has shown, the individual must always be subordinate to the team, to the mission, and what might be significant to one person can never take priority over the good of many."

"So Threat Analysis looks for sources of danger and deals with them before they become too dangerous?" said Ben.

"Exactly." Grant seemed pleased. "Imagine, for example, if a madman like Hitler could have been detected before he became influential — removed before he could find a following or gain any kind of power. Think how many lives might have been saved and how different the mid-twentieth century might have been."

"But could even Hitler be held responsible for atrocities he hadn't actually committed?" Cally frowned.

"An interesting point," admitted Grant, "and one that we'll perhaps return to in our next Ethics in Espionage lesson. But I want to finish today by showing you what Threat Analysis is drawing our attention to at the moment."

All at once, a plane descended through the wall and landed on the runway that had helpfully appeared across the middle of the classroom. The side of the plane bore the flag of a foreign power: red crosses on white, like blood on snow. The news reporter who had found her way to Grant's side filled them in. ". . . the first visit to the United States by a President of Wallachia in history. President Tepesch —" probably the tall man robed in black seeking sanctuary in a limousine before his features could be glimpsed — "will be involved in talks with the state department concerning his country's possible application for corpornation status."

"Wallachia? I can't even say it," grumbled Eddie. "Where the heck is that?"

The class became a map of Europe, the tiny state of Wallachia highlighted in the Balkans, like a small growth on the side of Romania. Stock footage showed densely wooded hills and valleys, wild horizons that seemed perpetually on the brink of night.

"The mainly agrarian economy of Wallachia —"

"That's farming to you, Ed," smirked Cally.

"— has suffered badly in recent years, and with the surrounding former Eastern European states either already granted corpornation status or in the process of application, President Tepesch may well have decided that his own people have little option but to follow suit."

A man with a beard and a bald head stepped from behind Grant. Words that hovered in midair introduced him as an expert in Wallachian affairs. "One of many, no doubt," grunted Ben.

"I would be surprised if President Tepesch were actively to seek corpornation status," opined the expert. "To do so would be to place the economic and therefore the social future of his country in the hands of American business interests, effectively losing his sovereignty over his own people. This would not sit well with a man who has always fiercely protected the independence of himself and his native land. It could mean the end of Wallachia."

"Terrific," said Eddie. "Call it something with a shorter name instead."

"Eddie," asked Lori critically, "don't you have any interest in the world around us?"

"Sure," claimed Eddie. "I went on vacation to England once. It rained."

And it was raining now in the classroom, but nobody was getting wet apart from a second news reporter who was standing outside the sheer concrete walls of what looked like a fortress or a prison. She was holding up a crimson-colored pill for her audience's inspection. "And this is one of them," she was explaining. "A Drac tab. It contains the most addictive and dangerous new drug to plague the streets of America for generations. Just one of these can ruin a life — reduce the new addict to an existence of total dependency on the drug. It's happening already in our major cities, and the numbers of affected are increasingly alarming. The side effects of Drac are severe, but the most worrying thing is that there seems to be no cure for the addiction yet, no way of weaning the victims off the drug."

Ben didn't seem to share the reporter's concern. "Nobody made them take Drac in the first place. You make choices, you take the consequences."

"Not everybody's as strong as you, Ben," said Lori.

"Or rich enough to be able to afford to make choices," added Cally.

"Yeah, yeah," scoffed Ben. "It's always someone else's fault."

The reporter meanwhile had been joined by an earnest-looking woman in glasses. "Dr. Stoker, you run the institute here and work with Drac addicts . . ."

"That's a hospital?" Eddie gazed up at the building's mighty and impregnable walls. "Who do they hire for nurses? SWAT teams?"

"I do," said Dr. Stoker. "Our work here is vital, not only in the hope that we can rescue these young people from their own addiction but also that we can perhaps find some general treatment or antidote that can counter the physical effects of the drug which, as you say, Mary-Beth, are severe."

"Let's hope so, Dr. Stoker," said the reporter, "before the evil of Drac can spread any further."

Spy High's Threat Analysis experts obviously thought that was an ominous enough note on which to finish. The rain stopped. The two women vanished. The classroom was, once again, simply that.

"So that's it?" Ben's resentment of Lori and Cally's earlier comments made him confrontational. "That's today's threat analysis? The president of a crackpot country down on its luck that no one's ever heard of and a few junkies living in luxury at the taxpayers' expense. All of a sudden, I don't feel so bad that we're down to four. I don't see anything here that's going to change the world."

"You don't think so, Ben?" Grant wondered mildly.

"No, sir." Ben could always be relied upon to stick to his guns (even when they were out of ammunition). "What kind of threat could Wallachia ever pose? And as for drugs and stuff, I mean there've always been junkies, haven't there? We've had crack and ecstasy and crystal meth and all that. It's hardly big news, and it's not like they don't get what they deserve."

Cally's mouth had fallen open. She finally found words to fill it. "I just don't believe you sometimes, Ben. I mean, ivory towers aren't big on windows, are they? They're lives aren't they? And every life is precious, isn't it, worth saving? I thought that was what we were here for — training for — to save lives."

"*Innocent* lives," Ben stressed. "Lives that are in jeopardy through no fault of their own. I don't rank junkies who turn to drugs 'cause they can't cope with the big wide world under that heading at all. They don't deserve our help."

Cally was on her feet now, shouting with indignation. "Who are you to judge, Ben Stanton? Who are you to decide which people 'deserve' our help and which people don't? I've never heard such ignorant arrogance."

"What," Ben responded with equal aggression, "and you think every last druggie on the street is one of life's little victims, do you, and personal responsibility doesn't come into it at all? Can you spell *naïve*, Cally?"

Eddie was glancing from Ben to Cally like a spectator at a

tennis match. Lori turned expectantly to Mr. Grant. He inclined his head.

"All right, that's enough, both of you."

It wasn't enough to disobey the senior tutor during class, but the way Ben and Cally continued to fume at each other, today was a close-run thing.

"I'm pleased you have strong opinions on this issue," said Grant. "I'm pleased you're both committed. But remember, Cally, Ben, nothing is ever quite as black or white as it seems. And to prove the point," he considered, "perhaps a little excursion is in order."

"Can we hope for Disneyland?" said Eddie, crossing his fingers.

"You know the first year teams are due to go on a field exercise this weekend," Grant continued. "Well, I'm afraid Bond Team won't be among them."

"What?" Ben might have just swallowed a Drac tab.

"What, sir?" corrected Cally. Though she and the others didn't seem too pleased, either.

Grant was oblivious to the objection in any case. "Mr. Deveraux doubts the value of sending an understaffed team on a field exercise, but I doubt the usefulness of having you remain at school kicking your heels. Therefore, given the depth of feeling that Ben and Cally have just expressed . . ."

Ben guessed what was coming. He muttered to himself. "I don't believe it."

". . . a visit to the Stoker Institute itself might be helpful. Perhaps some exposure to the realities of Drac addiction might lead both of you to moderate your views."

But from the expression of both Ben and Cally's faces, Mr. Grant would have been ill-advised to hold his breath.

* * *

"Jake Daly." Kim Tang said the words like they should be R-rated. "Hmm, nice name. Kind of strong, dark, and attractive. Suits you, Jake." She shook his hand as they took their seats at Gaudini's.

"It's a pleasure to meet you, too, Kim." Jake smiled.

"And polite as well." Kim turned to Jennifer. "Any more like him back at this Deveraux Academy, Jen? Maybe I should apply for the next semester, after all."

"Jake's pretty much one of a kind," Jennifer said, aware that he was blushing.

Kim sighed. "I had a feeling he might be."

They paused as Mr. Gaudini brought over their drinks. "On the house," he said. "And once again, I must apologize for the previous disturbance." Evidence of which was now covered over while a pane of glass was awaited. "The times we live in." Gaudini departed with a dejected shrug.

"Well," said Kim to Jake, "I just hope you've come to take Jennifer back to your fancy school, and the sooner the better."

"'Fraid not," Jennifer said coldly. "Jake's come to help me find the man who killed my family."

"You're still obsessed with that?" Kim was dismayed. "Even after we nearly got our throats ripped open by a couple of Dracs?" She briefly explained what had happened to a blank-faced Jake. "We were lucky. And they won't be the only Dracs around here."

"I handled it," Jennifer said. "You saw me, Kim. I handled them."

"Jennifer, listen to me." Exasperation crept into Kim's tone. "No, better yet, Jake, you listen to me and then we can work on Jen together. There's no law these days in Undertown, and even less order. Nobody in authority cares what happens here: the mayor, city hall, hardly even the police themselves. We're the dark secret that nobody wants to know about. So the gangs rule the streets of Undertown, and if you want to get by, you have to stay on the right side of the gangs or . . ." She faltered, realizing what she might have said.

"I know," said Jennifer.

"Yeah, sorry." Kim sipped her drink reflectively. "It's gotten worse since the Drac tabs started. Nobody's safe now, and nowhere. And there's a turf war, see, between the Serpents, who've always been here, and these new people muscling in called Wallachians. Something like that. It's the Wallachians who're peddling the Drac, trying to take over. And the Serpents don't like it, and they're fighting back. And everybody else is caught in the middle. You know, with like *Innocent Bystander* chalked on their foreheads. Innocent Victim. And every one of them would get out of Undertown if they could, Jen, only they can't so they've got to take their changes. But you can and you must. Tell her, Jake. You agree with me, don't you?"

"'Fraid it's Jen's decision," said Jake. "I'll support her in whatever she wants to do."

Kim shook her head and laughed bitterly. "They always say that good looks and brains don't go together."

"So I'm staying," Jennifer summarized, "and that's final. And the man I'm looking for is part of the Serpents, or he was when he murdered my family. I don't know his name, but he looks distinctive enough. Covered in tattoos like the scales of a snake."

If the description struck a chord with Kim, she didn't show it.

"He's been seen recently. Any ideas, Kim?"

Apparently not. "Look, if you want to risk your life on some misguided revenge kick that's up to you, Jen, but don't expect me to help you along the way."

"Not even for old times' sake?"

"Because of old times. Because I want us to both go on remembering them."

"Best friends forever, isn't that what we said? No matter what? We'd never let anything come between us, always be there for each other, always put the other first. Didn't we make a pledge?"

"That was a long time ago," said Kim.

"But didn't you mean it?" Jennifer pressed. "I did. Didn't you, Kim?"

Her friend sighed, fumbled for a cigarette, looked down at the table. "I suppose I did. I did, yes. Okay. You win. This guy with the scales or the tattoos or whatever, I can't help you with him." She raised her eyes to Jennifer's. "But I know where you'll find someone who can."

"My little bag of goodies," Jake said, pulling the carryall wide open for Jennifer to see. Shock blasters. Shock suits. Sleepshot wristbands. "Everything we need to put an end to the Serpents."

"You said it." Jennifer reached out.

Jake cautioned her. "But we're gonna do this right, Jen. Nothing wild. Nothing reckless. We're students at Spy High, and that means doing this by the book."

"Absolutely, Jake," said Jennifer as if she'd actually been listening.

It was a good night for the Undertown moon, which for once looked almost healthy — a night for lovers rather than vengeance. But Jennifer confined her thoughts strictly to the latter. Kim had given them a location not many blocks away where if you wanted drugs or any other illicit products from the Serpents, you could usually get them. A kind of one-stop illegal merchandise store.

Jennifer and Jake were going to close it down.

Above them the sky in the direction of Uptown was studded with advids, playing out lifestyle fantasies for anyone who could afford them, which excluded the entire population of Undertown, of course. If you lived here, you didn't have the money to look up. You had to confine yourself to looking down, down to the gutters where the Serpents squirmed. To places like Jennifer and Jake's final destination.

It was another empty shell of a building, bleak and uninviting, perfect for rats, of both the rodent and human varieties. The sharp-faced man (though he was barely that, barely older than herself, Jennifer judged) hanging around outside certainly fitted the part: He could have had whiskers. He ought to have been arrested just for the state of his appearance. Jennifer felt her fury and her frustration build inside her, and the urge to take them out on this wretched thing with the rat face. But restraint, discipline, she had to be controlled by these qualities. The spy who lost her temper was the spy who lost her life. She thought it wise to let Jake take the lead.

"Evening," Jake greeted Rat Boy as they made to walk up the steps and into the building.

"Where d'you think you're going?" Rat Boy blocked their path.

"It's a nice night," Jake observed conversationally. "My girl and me thought we'd make it a bit nicer and mix it with a few chemicals, if you know what I mean?" Rat Boy evidently didn't.

"Dope, you dope, we want to score. Heard this was the place to come." Jake produced a wad of notes and waved them like a flag. "We've brought the entrance fee."

"Should have said so first." Rat Boy displayed teeth that were as thin and sharp as the rest of him. "We'll be happy to oblige. After you. Second room on the left."

"It would have to be," Jake whispered to Jennifer. "Probably can't count beyond two."

The second room on the left seemed distinguished from the others only by the presence of a light and a trio of Rat Boy's comrades. Jennifer repressed a gasp. She was glad the light was dim. The black guy, the big Chinese, and the Caucasian with the complexion like freshly ordered pizza were the same three thugs who'd tried to mug her on her first night in Undertown. Small world. Small violent world. Jennifer stepped behind Jake.

"Lee," said Rat Boy. "Customers."

"Yeah?" The black guy swaggered up to Jake. "What are you buying?"

"Depends," said Jake, standing loosely, absorbing every detail of the room. "What are you selling?"

"Oh, everything." Lee flicked open a blade and wafted it in the air like some manic barber. "But any wrong moves, and the pain comes free. Maybe your lady knows what she wants."

Lee pushed Jake to one side. He saw Jennifer's face close up. Recognized it. "Hi," she said. "Guess this is a wrong move."

It was the same kick as before. And the same high-pitched response. Lee's voice went up, but the rest of him went down.

Jake whirled into action. A combination of blows took care of the Chinese guy, and when Pizza Face lunged with his knife,

Jake was more than ready. Dislocated before, the arm was probably broken now.

Rat Boy saw the way the fight was going and made a break for it. Out of the room, hurtling down the hallway, bursting out onto the top of the steps. Jennifer followed, took calm aim with her sleepshot wristband. Got him right between the shoulder blades. Rat Boy pitched forward. He hit the sidewalk hard.

"So Lee," Jake was saying back in the room. The three Serpents were cowering on their knees. They hadn't really expected Jake to produce a shock blaster. "The pain comes free, does it? What about information?"

"Who are you? You're just kids." Lee's eyes were wide, wider still as Jennifer returned with her own shock blaster drawn. "Who's she? Are you Wallachians or something? I mean, it's cool if you are. We've been thinking of switching sides, anyway, right boys? Drac's cool, we can peddle Drac. Just don't kill us, yeah?"

Jennifer jabbed her shock blaster against Lee's head. "You miserable piece of slime. It's scum like you who mur —"

"Wait!" Jake's free hand squeezed Jennifer's shoulder. "*Focus,*" he warned. Jennifer looked at Jake, nodded tersely, redirected her blaster to cover the other Serpents. "No, Lee, we're not Wallachians. We're kind of freelance, but we're also kind of impatient as you've just seen. So talk and talk fast. We're looking for one of your guys with tattoos like the scales of a snake."

"Talon? You mean Talon?" Jennifer bit her lip. Blood in her mouth. A name. After five years she could put a name to her hate. "What d'you want him for?"

"That's our business," said Jake. "Yours is just to tell us where we can find him."

"There's going to be a big delivery of stuff," Lee said, eyes fixed on the barrel of Jake's gun. "Big delivery. Tomorrow night. Midnight."

"Well, there's something," grunted Jake.

"Talon'll be there. He's there for all the shipments."

"So exactly where is 'there'?"

"The docks. The pier. Pier Twenty. Pier Twenty at midnight. I swear on my mother's —"

"Don't!" Jennifer cautioned, green flames in her eyes. "Don't even think of saying that." It was fate. She had the idea of fate in her head now. Pier Twenty. The same number as her apartment. That was where her moment of destiny would come.

Lee was gulping on the floor. "Okay, okay. I didn't mean anything by it. It's just the truth. I told the truth. You're not gonna shoot us now, right?"

Jake smiled. "Not with this, no." He lowered his shock blaster, pulled back his sleeve to display his wristband, gleaming metal in the semidarkness. "With this, on the other hand . . ."

Sleepshot. Three shells. Three slumbering Serpents.

"But don't worry." Jake addressed his remark to the unconscious Lee. "When you wake up, it'll be in the comfort of a nice, cozy police cell."

"Too good for them," Jennifer gritted bitterly. "They should wake up in hell."

Jake frowned. When Jennifer was like this, he feared for her. "You all right?"

She squeezed her eyes shut, clamped her grief and rage

away. For the time being, at least. "I will be, Jake. Tomorrow. After midnight. After Pier Twenty and a little word with a man called Talon."

"D'you think Lee was on the level, that this Talon'll really be there?"

"Oh, yes," said Jennifer. "And so will we."

CHAPTER FOUR

It was his shot, and the setup couldn't have been easier. Roll the cue ball almost bashfully up to the eightball, a little kiss on the well-rounded cheek and into the pocket it would drop. No problem. Even someone with no arms could make this shot. Ben's entire future as a secret agent might be in jeopardy, but at least he could still beat Lori at pool.

Ben bent low over the table and made his play. The cue ball rolled up to the black. The eightball quivered toward the corner pocket, seemed to take a quick peek into its dark depths and decide against it. And stayed out. Ben said a word that did not appear in the Spy High instruction manual.

"Oh, Stanton, things really aren't going your way, are they? I'm so glad."

Ben didn't need to look up or around to know that Simon Macey, leader of Solo Team and a dominating figure in his top ten list of People He'd Most Like to See Atomized, was behind him.

Macey sauntered into full view in any case. He was grinning. It was like rigor mortis on a corpse. "What are you doing playing pool, anyway? Shouldn't you and, ah, what's left of Bond Team be getting ready for our field exercises? We are."

"Simon," Lori said, keen to defuse the confrontation before it detonated, "there are plenty of rocks on the ground. Why don't you go and crawl under one?"

Simon ignored her. "Oh, of course. I'd forgotten," he taunted. "You're not attending exercises, are you? Maybe Grant's worried he might lose the rest of you if they let you out of the building?"

"You might lose some teeth if you're not careful, Macey." Ben seemed to have a fresh idea of what to do with his cue.

"I've heard they're sending you to some rehab place instead, is that right? Always knew you'd end up in an institution one day, Stanton. Have fun, won't you? And don't hurry back." With a provocative wave and a humorless laugh, Simon Macey swaggered from the rec room.

"One of these days that guy is gonna push me too far," Ben glowered.

"Well, don't make it today," Lori advised. "And it'd be easier if you just ignored him, Ben. Simon only riles you because deep down, he knows you'll make a better secret agent than he will. We won the Sherlock Shield, didn't we?"

Ben grunted. "Yeah. But chances are, they'll be reclaiming that before long. There's probably a rule that says only teams with a full six members can hold onto it."

Lori sighed. Ben could sulk for the world when he felt like it. Most of the time, he came off as arrogant, even boastful, but the flip side of that was fear of failure. Lori knew the signs. Luckily, reinforcements were arriving in the shape of Cally and Eddie. They looked pleased, like messengers of good news. Lori hoped.

"Thought we'd find you both here," said Eddie. "Who won?"

"Oh, Ben's winning," said Lori.

"Jake's been on the videophone," Cally supplied excitedly.

"Has he now? Good for Jake." Ben stroked his cue like it might be getting a lot of extra work.

"He's found Jen. She's fine." Cally slightly corrected herself. "Well, given the circumstances."

"What circumstances?" asked Lori.

Cally explained. "So he wants me to do a computer check on this Talon, see if he's got a record and stuff. And maybe check out Drac and these Wallachians, too."

"Maybe he'd like to accompany us on our little excursion to the Stoker Institute," observed Ben acidly. "That should deal with the Drac."

Lori looked thoughtful. "Threat Analysis highlights the visit of the president of Wallachia while Jennifer and Jake learn that the Wallachians are involved in a turf war with the Serpent gang. They're pushing Drac, and the rest of us are off to discover its effects. Isn't that something of a coincidence?"

"Or what?" Ben seemed skeptical.

"I'm just remembering our trip into the Wildscape before Christmas," mused Lori, "how we just *happened* to be dropped so close to Frankenstein's lodge and everything that followed from that." She shivered at the memory. "All so convenient, wasn't it? From campfire to baptism of fire in one easy move."

"What?" Ben pressed. "You think there's an agenda here? You think Grant packing us off to Stoker is more than just an attempt to help me and Cally live together in perfect harmony?"

Cally coughed pointedly.

Lori considered. "I just think we shouldn't go into this visit with too negative an attitude, Ben. Whatever we learn, we might need someday."

"Yeah, right. Well, what I need now is a few words with Jake Daly, and none of them are likely to be pretty." Ben stabbed a finger at Cally. "When you videophone him back, Cal, let me know. I want to be there."

*   *   *

It was strange, Jake thought as he looked at Cally in the video-phone. Here he was in the empty shell of Jennifer's former home. There was Cally in the quiet sanctuary of Spy High, familiar furnishings glimpsed like old friends in the background. Another world.

"Is Jennifer there?" Cally was asking.

"No, she's at her aunt's," Jake said. "Did you find out anything about Talon?"

"Enough to know he's not a guy to play games with," said Cally, "except maybe Russian roulette." She glanced down as if consulting a piece of paper. "Talon. Real name Carter John Tracey. Mother: Marion Anne Tracey. Father: unknown. A petty criminal from an early age. Serial delinquent. Spells in youth institutions for terrorizing other kids, theft, burglary, property damage, etc. Oh, yeah, and once he hit a teacher over the head with a Bunsen burner. Doesn't say whether it was lit or not at the time."

"At least he was in school that day," noted Jake. "A real charmer."

"Was running with Undertown gangs before his teens," Cally continued. "Arrested as a member of the Serpents when he was fifteen. That's when he's first referred to as Talon. Seems the tattooing you told me about was started off by an older member of the Serpents as a kind of identification mark, a brand. Talon obviously liked it. It says here that his entire body — from the neck down, anyway — is covered in scalelike tattoos. Yuck." Cally wrinkled her nose distastefully. "I pity whoever had to research that."

"Anything more directly relevant to Jen?" Jake prompted.

"Not really. Talon rose through the ranks, became an enforcer around the time Jen's family was killed. Quickly gained a reputation for ruthlessness and is suspected of committing several gang-related murders. Never charged for any of them. Seems no one was prepared to rat on a Serpent, if you know what I mean."

"Scared," Jake sighed. "Too afraid to do the right thing."

"Yeah. But here's the really interesting part. All of a sudden, he just seemed to disappear — dropped right out of circulation. Rumors went around that he'd been killed by a rival gang, nothing proven. And now, just as suddenly, seems reports of his death have been somewhat exaggerated. Talon's back on the streets, and from what I can find out, Jake, he's now undisputed leader of the Serpents. We're talking someone who's seriously dangerous here. You think you know what you're doing?"

It was a question Jake avoided answering. "What about the Drac, Cal?"

"To me. Give it to me." A voice offscreen. Ben's. Cally seemed annoyed and looked like she intended to hold onto the videophone. She didn't get the chance. The picture shook as Ben snatched the videophone and thrust his own incensed features close to it, like pressing his face to a window.

"Ben," said Jake. "How's it going?"

"Like you care." Diplomacy was not Ben's strong suit. "Now listen, Daly, and I'm speaking as team leader now, you hear me? You've found Jen and that's good, but now you've got to come back, both of you preferably, but you definitely."

"Sorry, Ben, you'll have to speak up. Not receiving you very well."

"And Cally's right. This Talon character . . . you can't deal with him just the two of you. You've got to come back."

"What's that? Reception's really bad. I'll call you back later, Ben, all right?"

"Jake, don't you dare —!"

Jake dared. He switched the videophone off. He'd heard Ben Stanton rant plenty of times before. But while he'd never allow himself to appear doubtful in front of the team leader, there was no reason to resist a frown of uncertainty now.

Did he know what he was doing? He could talk about loyalty to a girl who was very special to him and how she needed him to be around to prevent her from doing anything stupid. He could talk about the importance of concerned citizens taking a stand against gang culture and the likes of Talon. He could even talk vaguely about it being too late to turn back now. But the bottom line, the short answer, was much simpler. Jake had to admit it, he didn't have a clue what he was doing or whether it was the right thing to do.

But he wouldn't have to wait long to find out.

As night fell, they prepared themselves. Jake had evidently packed with both eyes on possible conflict. They pulled on their shock suits, clicked their sleepshot wristbands into place, checked their radar-vision strips, their shock blasters, and their flash grenades.

"How did you get all this through airport security?" Jennifer asked.

"Oh, with a little bit of luck," said Jake. "The Spy High issue X-ray proof case came in handy as well. Don't leave home without one."

Jennifer laughed, but tensely. "Are we ready, then?" As if they were embarking on a polite Sunday outing. *By dawn, she'd have killed him. The snake-man, Talon, the murderer, he'd be dead before then and by her hand.*

"More to the point, are *you* ready, Jen?" said Jake. "Remember, cool head. No heroics. We're trained and we're good, but we're gonna be massively outnumbered. We watch. We wait. We think. I don't want you losing it the first moment you see Talon."

"I won't," Jennifer said. "I promise."

"All right." Jake accepted her word. "Then we're ready."

The cabbie who drove them to the docks made no comment about their dress, even though the silver of their shock suits was still visible beneath shapeless dark coats. He'd probably had plenty of strange fares in his time, and in Undertown, it was wise not to ask questions. Jennifer and Jake were dropped off where they'd requested. Job done, the cabbie left them to it, perhaps a little more quickly than the speed limit recommended.

The docks in this part of town had seen better days, or at least, Jake hoped they did. There was the stink of decay and desertion in the air. The piers waded into the black waters of the Pacific like old men drowning their sorrows. The few security lights were palsied and yellowed, like pensioners' eyes. The few security fences were as holed and hopeless as ancient net curtains. But none of it mattered. As in Undertown as a whole, any decent, law-abiding people who possessed the wit or wealth to do so had removed themselves elsewhere. Pier Twenty was the preserve of the criminals now. With two unexpected additions.

Jake and Jennifer threw off their coats and crept in the shadows toward the pier itself. Cover was good. "What would we do without crates and packing cases?" Jake whispered. It reminded him of a Spyscape scenario.

"There's no one here." Jennifer's voice was more anxious than Jake would have liked. "Lee was lying. This is a waste —"

Jake shook his head emphatically, pointed. Lights on in a warehouse building. Good lights, new lights. Lights ready for business.

And now voices, low and discreet but not low and discreet enough. Coming toward them. Jake and Jennifer slipped behind a crate. It was two men with pulse rifles. Obviously guards. Obviously neither highly paid nor highly intelligent. The first quality of a guard should be vigilance. These two weren't even looking for trouble. They found it, though. Sleepshot in the chest.

"Guess they won't be needing these for a while." Jake grinned, indicating the guards' guns. He slung one over his shoulder, and Jennifer followed suit with the other. "Add 'em to the armory. If we can pick a few more off like this, we'll be doing well."

In the distance, somewhere out to sea, there was the dull throb of an engine. Suddenly, a searchlight from the dark ocean came probing over the pier. "The shipment," Jennifer hissed. "Let's move."

They dragged the heavy, sagging bodies of the guards behind a crate and covered them with some loose tarpaulin lying there. The engine grew louder. A launch. Whatever was going to happen, it was going to happen soon. More voices, raised in harsh laughter, as the warehouse door opened and another group of men came out onto the pier. Six, eight, with maybe more still inside.

"Jake," Jennifer urged hotly. "Let's *move.*"

"Not yet." *Cool head.* Jake was thinking. "Not until we know numbers."

They could make out the launch now as it pulled up alongside the pier. Greetings were exchanged between those onboard and those on shore. Their enemies had probably just doubled their strength. Jennifer had a glazed, distant look in her eye.

"Let's go to radar vision." With practiced swiftness, Jake wrapped the strip around his head, covering his eyes. It clicked where the two ends met, hardened, and allowed Jake to see in all directions at once. "Jen? Do it."

"What?" Vacantly. "Oh, yes." She fumbled with her own radar vision, finally fitted it. "I'm seeing the circle."

The launch was moored, the engine shut off. There was movement between the boat and the pier. A transaction was taking place. Cargo was being unloaded.

"Is he here?" Jennifer was straining at the leash. "Is he here? Let him be here."

"Jen, calm down. Think like a spy. Cool head." Empty words, Jake realized. If only the rest of the Bond Team were present. Jennifer was losing it. They were in big trouble unless he could do something.

More powerful lights blazed on, lining the pier. A final — Jake hoped — group of Serpents emerged from the warehouse. In the lead, as if preparing the way for the main attraction, a man whose eyes were hidden by dark glasses, not an entirely necessary accessory at this time of night. Behind him were slouched pulse-rifled bodyguards. Then, last of all, a man taller than any of the others, and muscular, too, like a body builder. A man who strode out with cruel authority, who was evidently oblivious to the midnight temperature, naked to the waist. All the better, perhaps, to show off the tattoos that laced his skin like the cold scales of a snake. Cally's records needed to be updated. Now Talon was tattooed over his shaven head, too.

What might have been human in him was subsumed by the Serpent.

A low wail issued from Jennifer's throat. The nightmare had awoken. Talon was so close to her. Her vengeance was so near.

The wail was a shout and a scream of hatred and fury.

"Jennifer —" She couldn't hear him, couldn't heed him.

Jennifer Chen burst from behind the shielding crate. "Talon! Talon, you —!" Her words were as violent as her actions. She was hurtling toward the Serpents on the pier, her shock blaster blazing from one hand, the fallen guard's pulse rifle from the other.

"Jen, no!" Jake could have been talking to the wind.

She had the element of surprise. Her initial pulse blasts went unanswered, the setting for materials punching holes in the pier and the warehouse wall, light spilling from the latter like white blood. Crates exploded like mines. Some of the Serpents sprawled for cover. Some of them. But not Talon.

And the element of surprise did not last for long.

The Serpents returned fire, Talon yelling orders. Pulse blasts tore up the ground in Jennifer's path. She didn't seem to care. She went on. It was as if she thought herself invulnerable, as if her righteous revenge would protect her from harm.

The real world didn't work like that.

Jake raced to Jennifer's aid. Firing his own shock blaster. Diverting some the attention from Jennifer. Who was now picked out by the spotlight from the launch, frozen in the brightness, trapped, exposed. An easy target.

Jake threw himself at her as the very air seemed to catch fire. He felt a searing pain in his left arm, but on missions, you couldn't afford to feel pain. Of any kind.

They tumbled to the ground, rolled toward relative safety. Wooden crates splintered and crackled as the Serpents' attack continued.

"Jen?"

"Let me go, Jake! He's here! Let go of me!"

She writhed beneath him, accidentally struck his left arm. Jake recoiled. Jennifer scrambled to her feet. He had maybe one chance left to keep her alive.

A flash grenade.

Jake lobbed one into the air. High. It wouldn't reach the Serpents. It wouldn't need to. The flash grenade detonated in the sky, and a light like white fire, like the heart of an atom bomb, engulfed the pier. The Serpents screamed. Light like white-hot pokers in the eyes, stabbing, blinding, crippling. Their radar-vision strips protected Jake and Jennifer, and the effects of a flash grenade were only temporary, but temporary might be long enough.

Jennifer was certainly exploiting her new advantage, evading the wild, ill-directed fire of the Serpents with ease. Jake pursued her, covered her as best he could. There was Talon, gouging at his eyes as if he might do better to yank them out and start again. And Jennifer was bearing down upon him with the force of fate.

A warning *whoosh* sounded from the boat. An explosive shell, randomly aimed. They got lucky. The pier ahead of Jennifer erupted, and she was flung sideways in the blast, sent smashing against a wall and then the ground. Groggily, she tried to rise.

"Jen!" Jake's blood thudded in his ears. There were sirens, too, like the cries of metallic beasts, and the screeching of tires.

Behind him, Jake could see the police arriving; in front of him, the departure of the remaining Serpents. The launch's motor was revving up once more. Talon and the man with dark glasses bundled aboard.

A dazed Jennifer instinctively realized what was happening. "He's getting . . ." She willed her body to move. It wasn't obeying. "Jake . . . stop him . . ."

"It's no good, Jen." He felt like a traitor to say so. "Not now."

The launch was already beyond effective range of their weaponry. There was nothing they could do.

"Please, Jake," Jennifer pleaded, staggering to her feet. "He can't get away . . . not again . . . please . . ."

The cops were close. Jake didn't fancy explaining himself to them. Deveraux would keep them out of real trouble, but it might mean a forcible return to Spy High. And he wasn't ready for that just yet. "Come on, Jen." There was still time for their own vanishing act. "Let's get out of here." She nodded, her strength returning. And as they melted into the shadows, he couldn't help but wonder: *Who could have called the police?*

Jake might have had some idea if his radar vision had also included telescopic sights. Then he might have seen as far as the dark limousine parked in the street beyond Pier Twenty, a vehicle noticeably at odds with the general seediness of the area. And if he'd been able to peer through the black one-way glass, Jake would have discovered the presence of a man like a heavily whiskered bull. He seemed to be fuming, and when he spoke, his voice was thick with a heavy Eastern European accent.

He addressed a figure on the videoscreen set into the seat in front of him: ". . . only partially successful, my prince. The local law enforcement appeared, but the intervention of the two young people thwarted our full intent. No, at least our own role in events remains hidden. . . . No, I have never seen them before. But they cannot be acting alone. Their weaponry, their clothing . . . Yes, I have already taken steps. They will be followed, and they will be watched . . . Yes, my prince. And when we know more, then we will act."

CHAPTER FIVE

By the time they reached the refuge of the apartment, Jennifer was all but hysterical. Her eyes were red raw, and her face streaked with tears like old scars. She was shaking, couldn't seem to stop. Restlessly, she roamed the room, a prisoner in a cell. It was Talon. He was tormenting her now more than ever.

"I had him. I had him." Her hands made violent shapes in the shadows. "He was . . . in my grasp. I was so close. But I failed. Failed. I'm worthless." She thumped the wall in her help-lessness and frustration.

"It wasn't your fault, Jen." Jake moved to embrace her. "We did our best. There were too many of them. We couldn't have . . ."

But Jennifer wasn't listening, turned her back. "Mom, Dad, I'm so sorry." She dropped to her knees, hugged herself, rocked herself back and forth. "But why did you leave me alone?"

Then, as he saw her bowed and vulnerable, Jake felt his heart squeeze within him like a fist. He could scarcely breathe, and he knew he could never survive without her. He knelt be-fore her, raised her face to his. "You're not alone." His tone left no doubt. "You're not, Jen. I'm here. With you. I'll always be here. I promise."

"Jake?" Was he getting through? There was bewilderment in her eyes. He could drown in her eyes and be grateful.

"And we'll get him. He might have escaped tonight, but there'll be other nights. We won't stop until we've got him. You hear me, Jen? Nothing is going to stop us."

"Jake, your arm. What happened to your arm?"

Jake looked down at his left arm in astonishment. At the ragged tear in his shock suit. Blood was still welling from the bullet wound in his flesh, the wound that he'd virtually forgotten about. "It's nothing," he said. "It's superficial."

"But it was my fault," Jennifer said in dawning horror. "You told me to keep cool, but as soon as I saw Talon, I lost my head completely. I could have got us both killed."

"But you didn't. We're both alive. That's all. It doesn't matter what didn't happen."

"Jake, you could have died because of me."

"*For* you, Jen. There's a difference." He held her hands, felt their warmth, their life. "And I'd do it. If it came to it. I'd die for you."

"You would?"

"'Fraid so."

Jennifer smiled for the first time that night. "Then I guess I'd better be more careful in the future."

They laughed then, and they held each other. Talon and blood and murder — none of it seemed to matter, all Jake knew was that he never wanted to let Jennifer go. As long as they were together, he thought, they were strong. As long as they were together, they were safe.

The Stoker Institute rose from the top of a hill like a castle of old, though not so much to keep invaders out, perhaps, as to keep its occupants safely in. The gray concrete walls seemed to glower at Bond Team as they were driven toward them, as if resentful of their arrival. Lori was reminded of old horror movies where the mad scientist dwelled in his lonely castle, carrying out inhuman experiments until it was attacked by a village of peasants brandishing torches. *If those films ever became fashionable again,* Lori thought, *a location manager could do worse than to bear the Stoker Institute in mind.*

Iron gates like a more advanced portcullis, opening grudgingly on their driver's presentation of his credentials. Natural light switched to artificial as the car entered the body of the building. It was probably psychological, but Lori already felt herself suffocated in here, trapped. A smell of disinfectant hung in the air like fog.

The earnest woman in glasses whom the students had already seen during their History of Espionage class was waiting to greet them. She looked only marginally pleased to be doing so. The man who accompanied her, big, uniformed, a head like a rock badly sculpted by a child, appeared distinctly unhappy.

"I'm Dr. Stoker," the woman said. "Miriam Stoker. I'm the director of this institute. You must be the students from Deveraux Academy." Ben, taking the lead as always, admitted that they were and performed the introductions. Himself, Lori, Cally, and Eddie. "I'm pleased to meet you." Without conviction, Dr. Stoker offered her hand to each of them in turn. "This is Officer Snow. He's our head of security here at the Institute."

I'll bet he is, thought Eddie. *I'll bet he munches boulders for breakfast.* "Tell him not to worry," he said. "We promise to behave ourselves."

"Stoker is essentially a treatment facility for drug abusers, as you probably already know," its director said, "but since we've begun to work with Drac addicts, we've had to make some changes, raise our security profile. For everyone's safety, you understand. Those in the latter stages of Drac addiction can seem a little hostile."

Officer Snow appeared to find something in his throat that needed expulsion at Dr. Stoker's use of "seem."

Cally, for one, was already employing her knowledge of psychological profiling to make deductions about Stoker and Snow. The doctor: on a mission of salvation rather than incarceration and skeptical of the need for security. The head of security: pretty much the opposite. There were clear tensions between them. If they were enemies, Cally reasoned, that'd be good, a weakness to exploit. As they were supposed to be allies, however, in any dangerous situation, it could be a problem. Still, what did it matter if Stoker and Snow didn't get along? What kind of dangerous situation could possibly arise during their two-day visit to the institute?

"It's not actual policy to admit nonprofessional visitors here," Dr. Stoker was saying, "though as Mr. Deveraux is a major financial contributor to our work, we are more than pleased to make an exception in your case."

Another artificial smile from Stoker. Not even that from Officer Snow. Bond Team wasn't wanted here. Cally didn't need to have had any lessons in psychological profiling to recognize that. And judging by Ben's lame "We're pleased to be here," the feeling was mutual.

Dr. Stoker showed them to their rooms, separate accommodations for boys and girls, as a foretaste of showing them the institute.

"I can't believe it." Ben subsided onto his bed and clasped his head in his hands. "This is such a waste of time, such a total waste of time. What are we even doing here?"

"Not looking on the bright side, that's for sure." Eddie

wandered over to the window. "Did you bring any clingskin, Ben? Maybe we can shinny out the window and find a club or something, or at least somewhere that doesn't reek of Lysol."

"Anywhere but here," moaned Ben quietly.

"Nah, scratch that." Eddie rapped his knuckles against the window in disappointment. The resulting sound was of metal, not glass. "It's a Viewscene, a hologram. 'Fraid we don't even have a proper window at all."

"Suits me, Ed. Till we leave this hole, there's nothing I want to see."

But Ben wasn't getting a choice. Dr. Stoker soon returned to take her visitors to the Treatment Wing. Officer Snow evidently had nothing better to do than accompany them. "Me and my shadow," whispered Eddie.

"Since the advent of Drac," Dr. Stoker said, "we've moved our other patients, those with treatable addictions, either to other parts of the institute or elsewhere altogether. The Treatment Wing is now entirely devoted to our work, our pioneering work, if I may say so, with Drac addicts." If Stoker was expecting applause, what she got was another cough from Officer Snow, who really ought to get his throat checked out by a doctor, Cally thought.

"Sure they haven't rechristened this the Alcatraz Wing?" Eddie wondered.

More checks. More security. Bars spread to doors and windows like a contagious disease. Surveillance cameras everywhere like nosy old women. And guards in the same uniform as Snow (though bearing a different badge). Guards armed with stun rods. Guards who seemed reluctant to let the little group past and into the Treatment Wing itself. "Maybe they know something we don't," Eddie whispered to Ben, but his teammate seemed intent on demonstrating a haughty and total disinterest.

Cally, on the other hand, had plenty of questions. "What can you actually do for the addicts, Dr. Stoker? I mean, I've heard that there is no cure for Drac addiction, that people can't be weaned off the drug in the normal way."

"I'm afraid for the moment that is true," acknowledged Dr. Stoker, but pleased by Cally's interest. A kindred spirit, perhaps. Someone who wanted to help, who might even share her vision of redeeming the poor, lost souls of the addicts. "However, we are making some kind of progress, let me show you."

She led them into a room that closely resembled a conventional hospital operating room. "Any chances of a few nurses, eh, Ben?" nudged Eddie.

"What we do know is that Drac attacks the bloodstream," Dr. Stoker said. "It partly has the effect of inducing the symptoms of anemia in its victims, whose skin swiftly becomes frighteningly pale, the first really identifiable sign of addiction. But at the same time, Drac seems to infect the very blood itself somehow, to poison it, leading the victim to see out, unfortunately almost always violently, the means of cleansing and purifying him or herself. As I say, though, we are now beginning to be able to slow the process by a sustained program of blood transfusions, replacing the infected blood with biologically treated whole blood. Even this only works with those in the very early stages of addiction, and the vast majority of our patients here are too far advanced for transfusions to be in any way effective. But we're constantly refining our techniques."

"What if you were able to treat someone almost immediately after they'd taken Drac for the first time?" Lori asked.

"Then I think we'd have a good chance of saving them," Dr. Stoker said. "But sadly that hasn't happened yet."

"Dr. Stoker?" Eddie fluttered his hand. "What you were saying before. The addicts seeking to cleanse and purify themselves. I mean, what do they do, then? Douse themselves with deodorant?"

"Eddie!" Lori and Cally looked hurt. Officer Snow stifled a snigger. Ben preserved his supreme indifference.

Dr. Stoker regarded Eddie with the tolerant pity of the visionary accustomed to the mockery of the ignorant. "Not quite — Eddie, isn't it? Not quite, Eddie. No, to cleanse their own blood, they attempt to carry out their own transfusions."

"Their own . . . ?" Eddie wished he hadn't been so smart now. He had a feeling he wasn't going to like what was on Dr. Stoker's lips.

"They attack other people, Eddie. They open them up. They drink their blood."

Eddie winced. "What, like vampires?"

"Why do you think the drug has come to be known as Drac?"

"Yuck, that's so gross." Eddie felt around his throat as if to check for puncture marks. "So why do they take the stuff in the first place?"

Ben and Cally looked at each other pointedly.

Dr. Stoker sighed. "That's a very good question. Perhaps we'll let some of our patients tell you themselves. Let's go to my office."

Dr. Stoker evidently recorded her interviews with the addicts, and judging by the meticulously catalogued rows of discs in her office, she must have spent most of her waking life interviewing. She selected two examples to play while her four visitors settled into chairs.

The pale, ghostly face of a girl barely older than the Bond Teamers stared at them from the videoscreen, eyes wide, almost swollen, almost colorless, shoulders hunched, but shuddering as if exposed to the Arctic.

"This is Karen," introduced Dr. Stoker.

"It wasn't my fault." The girl shook her head in sudden twitches. "I knew it was wrong. I knew I shouldn't take it. But I was so unhappy, my life was so pointless, nothing I did ever seemed to matter, and nobody cared. And they told me I could forget all that with Drac. They said Drac would make me feel good. I mean, like someone important. And I wanted to feel like that, even just once." A thick, bitter smile exposed the girl's teeth. "Don't feel so good now. But they made me take it. It wasn't my fault."

Cally glanced toward Ben with an expression of vindication. Ben frowned.

The second disc contained images of a young man, early twenties, perhaps, a shock of hair like congealed night crowning glaring features and a vicious leer.

"And this is Sandon," Dr. Stoker admitted, almost with guilt.

"Is that what you want, Doctor, a sob story?" A cold chuckle. A grotesque spasm as the Drac plucked at his muscles. "Well, don't waste your sobs on me. Save them for someone who cares. Me, I *like* Drac. It's made me strong. You don't know how strong, Dr. Stoker. I can do anything. Maybe even live forever. You're wasting your time with me, I'm telling you now. I'm not a victim. I'm a king." Sandon thrust his icy features toward the screen. "A king."

Ben's turn for the told-you-so look, Cally's to be disappointed and sullen.

"Every addict is different," said Dr. Stoker, "but here, we treat them all the same, from the basic assumption that whether they recognize it or not, every one of them needs our help. Actually, as it happens, I have a counseling session soon —" she checked her watch — "with a group including both Karen and Sandon. I wonder if any of you would like to sit in on it?"

Eddie felt he'd sooner sit in on the worst parts of World War II. Ben stared with sudden interest at his feet and even Cally avoided meeting the doctor's inquiring eye.

"I'd like to," volunteered Lori, surprising herself almost as much as her teammates. But she was recalling what she'd said back at Spy High. It would be wise to learn as much about Drac as they could.

"Would you?" Dr. Stoker said, gratified. "Excellent. I'm sure you'll find the session most memorable."

"I hope so," said Lori.

If Kim Tang was honest, she wasn't entirely surprised when she arrived at Jennifer's old apartment to find Jake Daly with his shirt off. The bandage around his arm, however, that was another matter. "What happened to you?" she asked.

"Oh, a little accident."

"Is there anything I can do?" she grinned meaningfully.

"I don't think so, Kim." Jennifer walked in from another room and crossed pointedly to Jake. "We're doing just fine as we are, isn't that right, Jake?"

"That's right, Jen," echoed Jake. "Thanks for the offer though, Kim."

"And for giving us a starting point. With the Serpents, I mean." Jennifer's tone hardened. "Not only do we now know the name of the man who murdered my parents and brother, but we've seen him in the flesh. And given him something to think about."

"What do you mean?" Kim wasn't following.

"We kind of gate-crashed something of a Serpent party last night," Jake said. "Down at the docks. Made sure it went out with a bang."

"That was you?" Now Kim was in disbelief. "That was you two?"

Jake narrowed his eyes suspiciously. "You seem to know something about it, Kim."

"I do. Yeah. That's what I came to tell you." She regarded Jake and Jennifer with renewed interest, a mixture of admiration and fear. "The word's out on the street that a shipment of Serpent drugs was badly disrupted last night. Word is that it was the Wallachians and plenty of them."

"Well, word's wrong," snapped Jennifer. "It was me and Jake, and no one else until the cops showed up."

"But . . . word is the attackers had guns and grenades and stuff. Professional."

"And?" Jennifer said.

Kim thought of herself and Jennifer, little girls, playing in this very room with their dolls. She thought of Jennifer's pretty, laughing face, her small hands clapping. The teenager she saw before her now, with her dark, intense boyfriend, was another person entirely. But then, Kim supposed grimly, so was she. "What kind of school is it you go to exactly?"

"The kind you don't need to worry yourself about, Kim," said Jennifer.

"But I still don't think you understand what you're getting yourself into," Kim persisted. "Talon isn't simply going to forget

what happened last night. If he finds out it wasn't the Wallachians, he'll come looking. And if you're not careful, Jen, he'll come
looking for you."

"Good," said Jennifer coldly. "I hope he does. I want him to."

"Jake," Kim appealed, "you're getting in over your heads
here. Trust me."

Jake frowned. He was missing something, a sixth sense
warned him. Something was passing him by. But he didn't know
what. And maybe he was wrong, anyway. Jennifer certainly
didn't appear concerned.

At the counseling session, Lori sat between Dr. Stoker and another white-coated member of staff called Dr. Irving, a young
man with a permanently queasy expression, as if he'd recently
eaten something that was upsetting him. The addicts themselves, some half-dozen of them, including Karen and Sandon,
completed a circle of chairs. They were all the same age, all pale
and gaunt, like they were wasting away, and they all twitched
and shook as if something inside them longed to seize control
of their bodies. Dr. Stoker seemed serenely oblivious to any possible danger from that source, however. Not that security was
taking any chances. There was a guard on the door.

"Now, whose turn is it to start today?" Dr. Stoker com-
menced. "Karen, isn't it you?"

The girl Lori recognized seemed to be practicing the crash
position for the next time she took to the skies. She shook her
head slowly and dismally. "Oh, Dr. Stoker . . ."

"I want to say something!" Stridently. Aggressively.

"Sandon, it's not your turn," Dr. Stoker pointed out gently.

"Remember the rules. Each of us speaks in turn, and it's Karen's turn."

"They're your rules, not ours," griped Sandon. "We don't have to accept them. We can do what we like, and I want to know what she's doing here." Not only did Sandon jab at Lori with the blade of his finger but he got up, too, took an intimidating step forward. Was he going to attack? The guard seemed to think so, drew his stun rod, and advanced toward the group.

Dr. Stoker waved him back, stilled Sandon with her other raised hand. "The rules are for everyone, Sandon. The rules are to prevent outbursts like yours and to keep order. And one of these rules is that we remain in our seats during therapy. If you wish to continue as a member of this group, Sandon, I suggest you resume yours."

Lori observed the addict, thought that every fiber in his body was aching to pounce at Dr. Stoker, and on her. That he could restrain himself only barely, only by a huge effort of will. But restrain himself Sandon did, returning sullenly to his seat.

"Thank you," Dr. Stoker said, "and to prove my appreciation, Sandon, I'll answer your question even though it was asked out of turn. Lori is here as an observer. She's here, because she's taken a keen interest in yourselves and your condition."

"Well, good for Lori," growled Sandon sarcastically. His eyes revealed only hostility. Lori was rather grateful for the presence of the guard. She was beginning to wonder how long the therapy session lasted.

"Now, Karen," Dr. Stoker resumed, "is there anything you'd like to share with us today?" Voice thick with caring.

The girl swayed, gyrated on her chair, seeming deeply troubled. "Oh, Dr. Stoker, I can't . . . not in front of everyone . . ."

"You can, Karen, of course you can," cooed the counselor. "We're all friends here. We all want to help."

Karen bent forward to an almost impossible angle, beckoned Dr. Stoker over. "Can't . . . not to everyone . . . but you, Dr. Stoker, I can whisper in your ear . . ."

"That's not quite in the spirit of the rules, Karen. The rules say we all —"

"Help me, Dr. Stoker. Please help me."

It was an appeal the good doctor could not resist. Her features wreathed in pity and wisdom and a deep understanding, Dr. Stoker stood up and crossed to the cringing Karen. Lori glanced at Sandon. He was laughing silently. The guard seemed a long way off at the door, and somewhere farther still, her friends, and Ben. She wished they were here. She wished she wasn't.

"Now, Karen, what is it? You can tell me . . ."

"Closer, Dr. Stoker, closer. It's a real big secret . . ."

Dr. Stoker was bending nearer. The addicts were clenching the arms of their chairs as though before an accident, a disaster. Sandon was eyeing the guard like a sniper. Lori braced herself for what she now knew was coming. "Karen?" said Dr. Stoker.

The girl lashed into action, whipped her arm around Stoker's throat. "I hate you! I hate you! I hate you!" Dragged her to the floor.

Dr. Stoker screamed. Her spectacles were struck from her face and shattered.

The addicts leaped. They smothered Dr. Irving, whose

queasiness now seemed like a prediction. The guard saw what was happening, but, in the moment he hesitated, Sandon was on him, clawed flashing fingers.

Lori's karate blow disabled the first addict to move for her, a kick floored the second. It was six to one. She could probably take them.

But they had hostages. Sandon with the guard, Karen clasping the distraught Dr. Stoker. "You stop, girl. You surrender. Or this is the last therapy session Dr. Stoker will ever take."

Lori didn't need a string of letters after her name to know that Sandon was serious. She had no choice. "Okay, okay. You win." The rule she lived by: Never endanger an innocent life. She prayed she wouldn't regret it.

"What? What are you talking about, no negotiations?" Ben demanded. "They've got Lori in there, and we've got to get her out."

Officer Snow was as unmoved as the rock he resembled. "They're holding Dr. Stoker as well," he said, not altogether without pleasure. "Which places me in charge of the situation. And I say we do not negotiate with junkies. Even if we let them go free like they're asking, what's to stop them killing their hostages later? No, there's only one solution to this problem."

"What's that?"

"My men storm the Treatment Wing, reclaim it by force."

Ben was aghast. "But what about Lori and the others?"

Officer Snow shrugged. "Guess they'll have to take their chances." He thrust his bulky face closer to Ben's. "Maybe next time, you kids'll stay at school where you belong. Now why don't you go back to your rooms and let the professionals do their job?" He turned his back on Bond Team.

"That guy's got a real helpful attitude," said Eddie.

"What do we do now?" Cally asked.

"Something," Ben gritted. "'Cause if we want to get Lori out of there safely, we're gonna have to do it ourselves."

CHAPTER SIX

"Keep watching, scumbag," said Jake. "You don't want to miss this."

The scumbag in question, a Serpent thug with a distinctive pattern of bruises about the face, looked like he might well want to miss it, but Jake's steady grip didn't give him much of a choice. He joined Jake and Jennifer in gazing up at the ramshackle building.

Which promptly exploded, bricks and flame showering the street, a sudden flare in the night. The Serpent cringed. Jennifer stood impassively, silently, the firelight dancing in her eyes.

"See? Instant interior redecoration," admired Jake. "One less safe house for you and your slimy friends to spread your poison from. And you go and tell Talon, there's no such thing as a safe house for him now. You hear me? What's your message?"

"Can't believe it." The battered Serpent seemed dazed in more ways than one. "You can't do this. You're just kids."

"Seeing is believing," said Jake. "Now tell Talon. No hiding place."

He shoved the thug to the sidewalk, watched him scramble to his feet and flee, pelting the teenagers with names over his shoulder as he ran.

"I don't know, Jen," with a purposeful grin, "we'll be getting a reputation soon if we don't watch out."

"He wasn't here." Jennifer had not moved. She watched the building burn with an arsonist's fascination. "He wasn't here, Jake."

"Don't worry about it." Jake worked his arm around her shoulders. "Sooner or later, he will be. Sooner or later, we'll flush him out. I promise."

Jennifer inclined her head. It would happen. Face to face with Talon and no means of escape. Then there would be a reckoning.

While a building burned in Undertown, Eddie and Ben were clambering onto the roof of the Stoker Institute. They wore radar-vision strips, sleepshot wristbands, and very determined expressions.

"Nice night for it," commented Eddie, breathing in the fresh air deeply. "Should have brought a couple of deck chairs up with us."

"Are you genetically incapable of seriousness?" Ben disapproved.

"Jokes are my way of coping with insecurities," Eddie said. "What's yours?"

"I don't have any insecurities," said Ben.

"Ah, denial. Gotcha."

"Eddie, keep your amateur psychology for someone who cares. Focus on the job at hand. Four people are depending on us, and one of them's Lori." Ben strode to the roof's edge. It was a steep drop to the courtyard below. "Check your strip's communicator. Cally, can you hear us?"

"Like you're whispering sweet nothings in my ear," came Cally's voice.

"Is that an invitation?" Eddie hoped.

"Just an observation, Eddie. And here's another. Snow's men are mustering at the entrance to the Treatment Wing. Judging from the hardware they're packing, they don't plan on conversation."

"Okay," Ben acknowledged. "Time to give them something to think about."

Cally nodded, not that her teammates could see it, not when they were on the roof and she was sitting in the relative comfort of her room, fingers gliding over the keyboard of her laptop like ice skaters in harmony. Cally's nod became a pitying shake of the head. If she survived the next few minutes, Dr. Stoker really ought to implement a radical overhaul of computer security. The institute's systems were like a bank with no safe. It had taken her seconds to hack in and minutes to wrest control from the original programmers. Deftly, Cally scrambled the codes on the security doors to the Treatment Wing. Officer Snow could pull rank all he wanted now, but he'd never get them open. Cally could almost hear his shouts of frustration.

She talked to Ben and Eddie: "All yours, boys. I think we can guarantee no interruptions."

Her teammates celebrated by jumping from the roof, legs together, arms by their sides, like human elevators on a one-way trip. Eddie was tempted to cry out, "Whee!" but doubted that Ben would be appreciative. Instead, he arrested his drop by thrusting his limbs against the building's wall. Eddie had drenched his hands and feet in clingskin. The adhesive clung to the concrete perfectly, which was probably just as well for Eddie's continued health. Ben was affixed to the wall alongside him.

"Monitor, Cally," he said. "Which way from here?"

Cally consulted the images on her screen. The schematics of the Treatment Wing were helpful, but the most vital information was being relayed to her from the block's spy cameras.

Not the obvious ones attached to the walls — the rioting Drac addicts released by Sandon had already torn those from their sockets like artificial eyeballs — but the second line of surveillance, the cameras inlaid into the walls themselves, that observed quietly and surreptitiously, showing Cally exactly where everybody was.

"The Therapy Room," she announced. "And they're all together. I count twenty-four addicts and all four hostages. There are four windows about fifty meters to your left and down two rows."

"On our way," Ben said. Four windows and only two of Bond Team. He and Eddie would have to be ultra-efficient. Course, if Jake and Jennifer had been with them as should have been the case, then they could have taken one window each and halved their number of targets. But then, if Jake and Jennifer hadn't gone AWOL, the rest of them wouldn't have found themselves in this situation in the first place. If Lori was harmed, Ben felt his rage building, if even one blond hair on her head . . . But anger was counterproductive in action. He'd be better advised to trust his training and skills and Eddie's, rather worryingly. He couldn't, wouldn't, let Lori down.

"Audio sensors fully operational, too," Cally was reporting. More implants in the Treatment Wing's walls. The authorities at Stoker not only got to see what their patients were doing every hour of the day, they got to hear it, too. And all for respectable therapeutic reasons, Cally half-convinced herself.

"Think about what you're doing, Sandon." An earnest, rational voice was speaking. Lori's. "There's no way they're going to let you out of here, no way you can win."

"You'd better hope different, girl." Another voice, bared and snarling like fangs. Must be a Drac. Must be Sandon. Cally saw him on the screen, hands on either side of Lori's head as if he meant to crush her skull between them. "'Cause if we lose, you lose. And I mean permanently."

"Oh, Sandon, why?" A bleating Dr. Stoker, blind without her spectacles, groping about on the floor as her counseling group stood around her and jeered. "Why? Why? I wanted to help you."

"You wanted to help yourself, Doctor," Sandon sneered. "To fame. To reputation. You never cared about us. You only ever wanted to feel good about yourself. So how do you feel now?" Much hilarity from Sandon's fellow addicted. "And what's keeping them? We want out, and we want it now. Before I get thirsty."

Cally didn't like the sound of that. "Are you in position yet, boys?" she hurried. "We don't have much time."

Outside on the wall, Ben and Eddie had chosen the two windows that were furthest apart, in order to create the largest possible cross-fire area. The windows were barred but it wouldn't matter. "In place," Ben said. "Ready when you are, Cal."

"What about you, girlie?" Sandon had returned his attention to Lori. "You want to help us, too? Why? You feel sorry for us?"

"Go to nitronails," Cally ordered.

As Sandon pushed Lori down onto a chair, others grasped her arms, yanked them back, tugged at her hair. Exposed her slim, bare throat.

"How sorry must you be now, girl, huh?" Sandon's mouth was wide like a pit of spikes.

Ben and Eddie peeled the explosive from their fingernails, commencing a mental countdown. Not thinking of Lori. Blocking her out. They each pressed a nitronail against a window bar.

"Blackout in three seconds." Cally from the communicator.

As Sandon stopped.

"Now!"

Lights extinguished with the press of a key. The Treatment Wing was plunged into darkness. There was a second of stark surprise.

The windows erupted inward, followed by a burst of sleepshot from both directions. "Get down! Get down!" Ben was yelling orders to the astonished hostages.

With radar vision, he and Eddie didn't need light to see.

They cut swathes through the suddenly panicking Dracs. The addicts didn't know whether to fight or flee.

Their indecision cost them as Ben and Eddie, equally ruthless now that the preliminaries were over, made each shell count. There were a chorus of shouts and screams and cries of despair. Eddie and Ben never made a sound.

"Ben!" Cally alerted him. "The one making a break for it. He's the ringleader."

Normally, Ben would have been in hot pursuit, gunning for glory. But he was already making for Lori. "Eddie, take him out!"

"No worries, leader man." Eddie bounded over fallen bodies, bright bursts of sleepshot still sparking from each wrist as he accepted the chase. Ben could mop up in the Therapy Room without him.

Sandon made the central corridor, raced along it. Nowhere for him to go, really. *Like a bowling alley*, Eddie thought. He went down on one knee, aimed. "And this for the championship. It's all down to Nelligan." At the last moment, Sandon stopped. He turned. He roared defiance. Eddie's sleepshot hit him right between the eyes. "Stee-rike! And it's all over!"

The lights went up. The security doors opened. Officer Snow and his men stumbled in, blinking stupidly as if they'd been brutally awoken from a deep sleep.

"Hi, guys," grinned Eddie. "Good to see the professionals doing their job. What do we think, Cal? Marks out of ten?" No answer. "Cally?"

"Oh, no. Oh, no . . ." Her voice suddenly seemed very small and lost.

Eddie didn't ask further questions. He ignored Snow calling after him, darted back to the Therapy Room. He saw the bodies of the slumbering addicts sprawling on the floor. He saw Stoker and the other two adult hostages standing sadly, like mourners at a funeral. And Ben crouching, cradling Lori in his arms, Lori unconscious, Lori with blood trickling from her throat like spilled wine.

Ben gazed up at him beseechingly. "Bitten," he said. "Eddie, Lori's been bitten."

Jake leaned back luxuriously in his chair, rubbed both hands over his belly and groaned with satisfaction. "That's about the best Chinese food I've ever eaten, Mrs. Chen. You ought to patent your sweet and sour recipe. You'd make a fortune."

"I'd love to . . . but I couldn't."

"Jennifer?"

"No, thanks, Aunt Li. Noodles go straight to my waistline,

and I wouldn't want to give Jake the excuse to cast his eye else-where."

"I only have eyes for you, Jen," Jake declared gallantly. "Waistline included."

"How very nice," observed Aunt Li. "Should we go to the living room?"

Jake was having a good time. It had been an excellent idea of Aunt Li's to invite him and Jennifer to dinner. "To get to know your young man," Jen had informed him was the reason. What-ever, the meal had certainly been an improvement over the end-less stream of take-out they'd lived on over the last few days. Jake supposed the visit was the equivalent of a new boyfriend being taken home to meet the parents, an impossibility in Jen-nifer's case. He glanced at her now, on the couch beside him. She was smiling, her face relaxed and happy. Maybe, if only for a while, she was forgetting Talon and her family's murder and the cold steel of revenge inside her. Jake hoped so. He squeezed her hand. Jennifer kissed him lightly on the lips as Aunt Li bus-tled at the sideboard. Yep, Jake was having a good time.

"It's here somewhere," Aunt Li was muttering, ransacking drawers. "I saw it about six months ago. . . . ah! There you are." Triumphantly.

"Oh, no," Jennifer groaned with a grin.

"What's up?" Jake watched Aunt Li withdraw a hefty volume in hard cream-colored covers from the mouth of the sideboard, like a dentist extracting a tooth. "You sound like you're in pain."

"I will be if that's what I think it is." Jennifer melodramati-cally covered her face in her hands. "Tell me you're not about to do what you're about to do, Aunt Li."

"Whatever's the matter, Jennifer?" Aunt Li scolded good-naturedly. She flourished the book like a trophy. "I thought your young man might like to see some of the family photographs."

"If he does, he can be somebody else's young man," Jennifer wailed. "Like now."

"Family photographs?" Jake repeated innocently. "I'd love to see them."

"I'm dead," Jennifer suddenly seemed to realize, and not too unhappily. "It's the end."

"Don't be so silly, dear," said Aunt Li. "There are some lovely ones of you here." She checked as if to make certain, laughed. "Look at this one, for example, stretched out on a rug with not a stitch of clothing on . . ."

"Maybe we should start with that one," leered Jake.

". . . and all of six months old."

"On the other hand, I guess we could skip it."

"I'm skipping them all, thanks." Jennifer hopped up, raising her hands in submission. "But if you're both intent on humiliating me, don't let my pierced and wounded heart stop you. I'll be in the kitchen doing the dishes. Let me know when it's safe for me to come out again."

"You'll know, Jen," Jake said. "The laughter will have stopped."

Actually, the photos of Jennifer made Jake feel more than amusement, significantly more. The tiny, often seemingly inconsequential moments from her life, quick frozen and preserved by the camera, like specimens in a museum of the past, seemed truly special, unique. Jake thumbed through the pages of the album like the leaves of a calendar. He was riding a time machine through Jennifer's childhood, a gurgling baby, a giggling infant, a serene and smiling little girl with the imprint of beauty already on her face. Blowing out six candles on her birthday cake as applauding parents looked on, seven candles, eight. But not nine. And with the album only two-thirds full, uncomfortably empty pages as blank as death. Jake looked to Aunt Li. Neither said anything.

"You're a good boy," she said. "I can see that, Jake. And you're good for Jennifer. I can see that, too."

"You think so?" Jake felt a flush of pride.

"Jennifer's life, it hasn't been easy." A sorrow settled on Aunt Li's brow like old age. "There's been so much tragedy, you know. She's had to cope with more than a person ever should. I tried to help her, even after my husband died, I did my best to help her through."

"I'm sure you did, Aunt Li," Jake said. "Jennifer's told me . . ." She hadn't, but the literal truth didn't seem important at moments like these. He squeezed the woman's hand comfortingly.

"What's this? What's this?" Jennifer appeared in the doorway. "Soon as I'm out of the room, you make a move on my aunt? Shame on you, Mr. Daly."

Jake laughed. "Guilty as charged. But I promise I'll make it up to you."

"You'd better."

"Ah, what a pleasant evening," sighed Aunt Li happily. "A pity that Kim couldn't come as well, though. It would have been nice to see her again."

"She did send her apologies, Aunt Li," said Jennifer, "but she already had a prior engagement. Knowing Kim, I bet it's with a boy."

* * *

The room was dark, somehow furtive, like a thief in the night or the evil in the hearts of men. The little light that glimmered from naked bulbs was filthy like an unwashed convict. It seemed reluctant to travel far, perhaps because it feared to illuminate the powerful man who dominated the room.

Talon didn't appear to care. Darkness, light — it was all the same to him. The reptilian scales seemed to crawl across his skin like illegible handwriting, like the chain mail worn in warrior times. His yellow eyes narrowed into slits. When he spoke, it was in a sibilant whisper and every word contained a threat. Had a forked and flickering tongue protruded from his lips, it would not have seemed unexpected.

"I trust your information is true," said Talon, with the clear implication that penalties would follow if it were not. The source of the information nodded her head vigorously, though her expression was pained and desolate. "Then the Serpents owe you a debt of thanks. The Wallachians are interference enough, without the added distraction of this girl and her ill-advised boyfriend. I don't actually think I can remember the incident you spoke of, but when you've — how shall I put it? — when you've disciplined as many people as I have, "obedient laughter from the thugs around the margins of the room, "then they all begin to merge together. Dead and then forgotten, that is the lesson of the world, a lesson that this Jennifer Chen should have learned. Now it seems someone is going to have to teach her."

"What are you going to do, Talon?" a frightened voice.

"Nothing, to begin with. You, on the other hand, my pet informant, are going to bring both Chen and Daly here, and you're going to do it tomorrow night. It seems that discipline needs to be applied."

"But Talon, you won't —"

"But?" The warning note in Talon's voice, like the rattle of a cobra. "Did I mishear? I thought you said 'but.'"

"No, Talon." Groveling. "I didn't. I didn't."

"Good. Then you know what to do."

"Yes, Talon," said Kim Tang.

CHAPTER SEVEN

Benjamin T. Stanton Jr. wasn't big on praying. Having been born into one of the richest and most influential families in America, he'd never needed to be. Self-belief and self-reliance, they were the Stantons' watchwords. What you wanted, you took, by yourself, for yourself, beholden to none. It was a philosophy that had always worked well for Ben before now, but then, before now, he'd never had a girlfriend bitten in the neck by a vampiric Drac addict. The Stanton fortune didn't seem to offer a lot of comfort at the moment. Indeed, as he kept a lonely vigil by Lori's bedside in the infirmary at the Stoker Institute, Ben wondered whether praying might not have something going for it after all.

If only he knew how to start.

Maybe with Dr. Stoker and the hope that the long string of letters after her name wasn't just for show but was proof that she knew what she was doing, because if she didn't . . .

"She's infected," Dr. Stoker had announced gravely. "Sandon's bite . . . the Drac has entered Lori's bloodstream."

"What can we do?" Ben had been desperate. He hadn't cared if Cally or Eddie or anyone else noticed. Lori was unconscious and bleeding. She was going to mutate into one of those . . . *creatures*. The idea was simply intolerable. "What can we do?" There had to be something. He had money.

"Pray we got to her in time," said Dr. Stoker. "Pray we can arrest and reverse the infection process before it's too late. Pray the transfusion works."

Bad blood pumped out. Good blood pumped in. Lori sprouting with tubes.

"Time will tell." That had been Dr. Stoker's diagnosis. "We have to wait for her to wake."

"But can't we . . . ? Isn't there anything . . . ?"

"You can pray, Ben."

And he'd been giving it some thought. Alone with Lori, his head bowed. A nurse appeared every now and then to check on the instruments, but Ben had sent Cally and Eddie away. It was his duty to keep watch over Lori and his alone. Stantons didn't shirk their responsibilities. They didn't share them, either.

"Lori," Ben murmured aloud. His eyes were closed. His hands, half-hidden between his knees, were together. That was the way he'd been taught to do it at school. "Be well. Make her well. Bring her back to us."

And someone was touching his arm, tenderly, tantalizingly. And not just someone.

"Lori, you're awake!"

Her eyes were open and gentle. A tired, weak smile. "You're not getting rid of me that easily," she whispered.

Ben pressed the button to summon Dr. Stoker. Lori was conscious. She was well. He'd have summoned a marching band if he could.

"You had me — us worried there, Lo, we thought we were going to lose you. We . . ." Ben gained courage. "I mean, I don't know what I'd have done. I couldn't have . . . you know."

Lori nodded slowly. "That's how Jake feels . . . about Jennifer. You mustn't be mad at him, Ben."

"You don't think so? No, you're right. You're right, Lo." Ben suddenly seemed to realize it. "And when we get back to Spy High, I'm going to do something about it. Deveraux said Bond Team had to be loyal to one another. Well, let's show him how loyal." Lori's hand squeezed a little harder. "We're gonna find Jake and Jennifer, and we're going to help them. I promise."

The vid call from Kim came while Jake was out cruising the streets for further information about the Serpents. He'd said Jennifer deserved a night off. But as soon as she saw her friend's face on the screen of her phone, she knew that something was about to happen, something shattering. Kim was tense, anxious. In all the years, Jennifer had known her, she had never seen Kim Tang afraid.

Times were changing.

"Jen? Thank God. Listen, I've got to be quick." Worried glances left and right, as if she expected to be attacked from either direction at any time.

"What's going on?" Jennifer asked sharply. "Kim, are you all right?"

"I've found someone, someone who can help you find Talon. I mean, actually get to Talon."

"What?" Jennifer's heart pounded.

"He's willing to talk, but he's scared, and it's got to be now. I can take you to him, you and Jake. I'd come to you, but I think I'm being watched."

"Don't worry. Where are you?"

"I'm at home."

"Give me your address. I'll be there as soon as possible. Just stay put, Kim."

"And Jake," Kim seemed keen to remind her. "You and Jake together, Jen."

"Yeah." A momentary poignance in her tone. "Me and Jake together."

"Jen?" Cautiously, even pleadingly. "You could still forget about Talon, you know. You could still just leave. Nobody would —"

"Address, Kim, and wait there."

Because it was impossible to forget Talon, here, in this empty, silent apartment, here more than anywhere. In some ways, Jennifer felt, Talon was here now, his influence, his evil lingering in the air like a stain that could never be cleaned, a mark that could not be erased. He moved in the shadows, dwelt in the darkness, a demon that needed to be exorcised.

And now it was time.

Mechanically, methodically, Jennifer climbed into her shock suit and donned her sleepshot wristband. She prepared herself for battle.

Should she wait for Jake? He wouldn't be long. He'd expect her to wait, insist on coming with her, insist on endangering his life for her. Like he'd done already. Jennifer remembered his wounded arm. It would still probably slow him down. She couldn't let him risk himself again for her. She wasn't worth it. Talon was her responsibility, hers alone. Jennifer Chen would face it bravely, whatever the consequences. For the sake of her family.

She wished she'd kissed Jake before he'd left, held him tightly, told him things that she'd never told another. It seemed she was always running away from Jake. But there was no alternative. Jennifer breathed deeply, as if the stale apartment air filling her lungs might sustain her purpose. She clenched her fists and closed her eyes.

Now it was time.

Jennifer's agitated mind only subliminally registered where it was that Kim was leading her. It had once been the entertainment district of Undertown, a parade of bars and clubs where people could go to drink and play and dream of a new life, or at least, for a few dollars here and there, forget their old one for an evening. "A den of sin and debauchery," Mrs. Chen had called it. "Anybody who goes there meets a bad end." Jennifer had been instructed to keep well away. She had done so, until now.

Advids glowed in distant skies, brightening the darkness for those who lived among the peaks and spires of Uptown. Here, though, in the lightless streets where the two girls crept, the clubs had been closed down. The revelers of former years were gone. There was no more dreaming.

Kim glanced back at Jennifer. She seemed nervous, had seemed so even before they'd set out. "No Jake? Where's Jake?" She'd been visibly upset by his absence, had almost refused to escort Jennifer anywhere all by herself.

"Jake doesn't know anything about this," Jennifer had said, calmly but firmly. "This is my business."

Grudgingly, Kim had been forced to accept the situation, to carry on with just the two of them. "Nearly there," she reported now. "If you want to back out, Jen, this is your last —"

"You're wasting your breath," Jennifer responded, never stopping to wonder why her friend seemed so reluctant to guide her to this informant. She'd not asked who he — or she — was, either, not that it mattered. He — or she — had information about Talon, and Jennifer would journey to the gates of hell for that.

In the event that the doors of a derelict club were sufficient.

"In here. Through here." Kim was physically trembling. "He's waiting, Jen . . ." She looked as if she was about to burst into tears.

Jennifer nodded emphatically for her to proceed.

The doors opened with an ease that Jennifer might have found surprising had she thought about it, given the building's general state of desolation, surprising and even suspicious. Well-oiled hinges, as though, for some purpose that had little to do with entertainment, the club was still very much in use.

But inside, it was pitch black, like walking into a grave.

Around them, the darkness was like a cloak concealing a terrible secret.

Kim turned one final time to her childhood friend, her face a desperate blend of sorrow and fear. "Oh, Jen, I'm sorry . . ."

And there was something cold in Jennifer's heart. Something like death.

"I've done it!" Kim was shouting. "I've brought her!"

"Kim, what —?" And words like *traitor* and *trap* occurred to Jennifer's startled vocabulary. Along with a phrase: *Too late.*

Lights blazed suddenly, as though a show was about to begin. Jennifer was momentarily dazzled. The cruel chuckles of bullies before a beating filled the room. And Kim was backing away, leaving her behind, leaving her alone.

Leaving her surrounded.

A noose of thugs. No informant. Only deception. Lee, Pizza Face, other thugs she recognized. Serpents. And older men, too, glaring at her, hating her. The feeling was mutual.

"Jennifer, isn't it? I understand you've been looking for me."

Talon. Jennifer felt her muscles twist and clench like a cramp. Talon, striding into the circle, arrogant, swaggering, feeling himself untouchable beneath the reptilian pattern of his tattoos. The nightmare of long years brought again to life.

"So." Talon smiled, and it was a sneer really. He was taunting her, and he was just a pounce away. The rage was in her, and it could not be denied. "Was there something you wanted to say?"

But before she took him, he had to know. Had to know why she was taking him down. "You killed my parents. You killed my brother."

"Really? How unforgivable of me. And how was it I missed making it a full house?"

"You left me." Jennifer's throat was thick with emotion. She could scarcely speak. "As an example. And you spoke to me. You told me not to forget, and I haven't. I've never forgotten."

"I take it you're not here to thank me for my generosity in leaving you alive."

"I'm here to kill you."

Talon's smile was a rictus of hate now. "Then let's get it over with."

Jennifer made to dart forward, but the Serpents closed in on her first. Talon stepped back outside the ring of combat. He was scared of her, but fear wouldn't save him. Nothing would. She was going to have to defeat a dozen or more lackeys before she could even get to him, but that didn't matter. It could be twice that number, and she wouldn't stop, wouldn't doubt, wouldn't flinch. Her whole life had been preparation for this moment, this one fatal confrontation.

She would not let her life mean nothing.

Jennifer's hands and feet lashed out, trained and deadly weapons, colliding with ugly Serpent flesh like hammers on meat. Her attackers were a blur of angry masks and flailing fists. They were many, but they were morons. They had no strategy. She could beat them all.

And all the time, Talon was prowling, observing, assessing.

In a corner, Kim Tang whimpered.

As another Serpent fell, Jennifer raised the stakes. Sleepshot was useless, in the press of bodies, but not her shock suit. Current coursed through it with an electric hum. Her kicks now flashed and sparked. Serpents screamed. Their blows, if they found her body at all, now coruscated with the suit's power, jolting volts of electricity through their arms and stabbing at their vitals. The Serpents were succumbing, smashing to the floor. The odds were evening.

Talon had seen enough. He clapped his hands. Those of his men still on their feet rushed away from Jennifer.

She was gasping for breath, but still strong. She could feel the spirits of her family with her, and they wouldn't let her fail. Their presence seemed very strong. If only Jake was here, too, she thought, but this was her fight and she would win.

Talon continued to applaud. The sound was hollow, sarcastic. "Well done, Jennifer. Very well done. Perhaps, if we had time, I might ask where you learned such skills, where you shop for clothes. But I'm afraid time is at a premium." He tensed, crouched, prepared to attack. "I have a war with the Wallachians to wage for the control of our streets. We have to defend our people against the scourge of Drac, and this petty feud of yours, young Jennifer, has annoyed me enough already. It ends. Now."

He threw himself at her, leaping like a lion.

Sleepshot. Take no chance. Remove the threat at once. Jennifer fired. Perfect aim at Talon's bare and tattooed chest.

The shell bounced off.

She kept her wits about her sufficiently to sidestep Talon's lunge, to try again and shoot at his back. Same result. No effect.

And Talon was laughing at her. "Ah, more toys, little girl. But I'm afraid that you, like many enemies before you, have made the mistake of thinking my scales are only of decorative value. True, they used to be simple tattoos, but no longer." He punched at his chest. "They're made of Kevlar weaving now. I have body armor stitched into my skin. A most painful procedure it was, too, but highly worth it, I think you'll agree." They were circling now, each waiting for the other to make the next move. "It'll take something a lot more powerful than whatever your puny bracelet fires to penetrate my skin. What else have you got?"

"Enough to take you out, Talon," Jennifer gritted, "with or without body armor."

With a yell of fury, she attacked. Her kick came with the force to break down a door. Certainly, Talon must have felt it. He rocked back on his heels. But he didn't topple; he didn't fall. And he was laughing at her.

In Jennifer's mind, it seemed like he'd always been laughing at her. Her head was forever full of his scornful amusement as he'd killed her parents. She had to put things right.

A second kick. A third. A storm of blows like lightning bolts searing and scorching as Jennifer struck, and her shock suit sparked and the electricity flashed around Talon's armored form. But he resisted the pain he had to be feeling, and he had to be feeling it because finally he acted. Moved. Swiftly. Like a serpent.

Hands like manacles, like steel, like stone, seized Jennifer's ankle. They twisted. A shooting pain. Jennifer jumped and kicked upward with her other leg, caught Talon beneath the chin, suddenly and powerfully enough for him to let her go, to stagger him, to be rewarded by blood from his mouth as his teeth ground down on his tongue.

But he'd done damage. Injured her ankle. Any pressure on it, and she needed to scream. No way of kicking now, no leverage. New tactic needed.

No time. Enraged by the taste of his own blood, Talon was on her. His fists pounding down on her back. Electricity blazed. Jennifer felt her bones shake, her lungs bruise. Air gasped from her, and she couldn't breathe. Her elbow thrust back, deflected from Talon's scaled torso. She swung up with her arm again. Tried to throw him, get him off balance, but her ankle gave way and she crumpled. She felt a blow to her neck, an explosion in her head, behind her eyes. Then another in her side, into ribs as stiff and frail like the wooden bars of a cot. She felt them splinter.

Jennifer fluttered her free hand to defend herself. Talon grasped it as a murderous child squashes a butterfly. She felt her fingers crackle like burning twigs. Pain flared, and it was white like the heart of a furnace, and it seemed to consume her. There seemed to be nothing else.

Talon crushed her wristbands. Jennifer kicked lamely, weakly with her good foot. Then he clawed at the collar of her shock suit and ripped, tore, rent. The material came apart in his hands in a shimmer of sparks like a dying fire, and the mechanisms in it short-circuited, and it was just a garment again with no more shocks for Talon. It flapped open over Jennifer's vulnerable body like flayed skin.

He threw her from him like a rag.

"*Get up,*" Jennifer urged herself, like a coach for a losing team. "*Get up!*"

She heard hoots of derision from those surviving Serpents who seemed to sway around her. The world was reeling and it would be so easy to fall off, but she had to get up, she had to do something. But she could only see shadows, like someone with smashed spectacles.

One shadow seemed bigger than the rest. One shadow advancing on her.

She had to fight him. She had to fight him. *Stand up! Resist! Revenge!*

Talon unleashed a final, slamming blow, like a closing door at the end of life.

And it was funny, but Jennifer wasn't feeling the hurt anymore, and she wasn't where she thought she was, either. She was in a world of soft and soothing light like a warm bath and who should be here with her but her family: Mom and Dad and Little Shang, and they were laughing and clapping and pleased to see her. It had been a long time. They were hugging and kissing her, and there was no pain here, only light. And then her family was moving further, deeper into the light, and they were calling to her, calling her by name. They wanted her to go with them.

She wanted to go with them, too. But wasn't there something she had to do first?

It didn't matter. Nothing mattered now, nothing but the light and her family laughing and beckoning her on.

She felt strange. She remembered a name. Jake. She felt that she was going to miss that name.

But it couldn't be helped. Not anymore. No longer.

It was time, and the light was all around her.

She followed her family into its heart, and she didn't look back.

It was time.

"Jen? It's only me." Jake entered the apartment. "A waste of time tonight, I —"

The silence suddenly occurred to him. The absence.

"Jen? Are you in here?"

She wasn't. No message, either. No indication of where she might have gone or why. Jake froze. She'd never do anything stupid, would she, like run off after Talon without him? No, that'd be reckless to the point of suicide. Madness.

She'd probably popped out to see Aunt Li on a whim or something. Besides, her shock suit and sleepshot were . . .

"Oh, my God," breathed Jake.

And that was when he heard it, the engine of a car outside, gunning at reckless speed, roaring closer. And howls, hoots of wild laughter, like those of drunks but with a harder edge, a crueler tone. Drawing nearer.

She was in danger.

How he knew, Jake could never later explain, but he did know. The sound from outside, it had to do with Jennifer. She needed him.

He bounded down the stairs, heedless of the possibility of falling in the dark and breaking his neck. Jake Daly was not destined to die on a flight of stairs. He burst out into the street, ran into the road.

The car, a customized twentieth-century Cadillac, was careening toward him. It wasn't going to stop. Its speed increased. Its passengers made obscene gestures at Jake. At the last moment, he flung himself to one side, executed a perfect roll, and was on his feet again in the same fluent move.

In time to see them hurl something from the car.

Someone.

The body hit the road hard. Its momentum took it to the curb, but it made no further movement.

Jake groaned deeply, in his soul. He knew it was Jennifer, though he couldn't look. He knew she was dead, though he couldn't think. He knew who was responsible, and he *wouldn't* forget.

He knelt by the body, Jennifer's body, played his trembling fingers over the broken limbs, the gashed and wounded flesh. He cleared the thick black hair from eyes that had been the deepest green but which were now devoid of any color, glazed and sightless, like marbles. A trickle of blood ran from her parted lips. But no breath. Not the slightest, merest breath.

"Jen." Jake felt himself choking. "Jen."

He held her hands, and they were cold. They'd always be cold now.

Jake's head bowed low, and his grief tore itself from him in wracking, shuddering sobs. He didn't care if anyone saw him, didn't care about anything. Not now. Not ever again.

He'd lost her.

CHAPTER EIGHT

They were flown to Los Angeles in Jonathan Deveraux's private jet, complete with full-sized beds for anyone who wanted to sleep, state-of-the-art holo-helmets for anyone who wanted to let their imagination run riot, and a well-equipped gym area for anyone who wanted to keep fit while in the air. The members of Bond Team availed themselves of none of these facilities. They sat upright, and they stared ahead of them, and they scarcely said a word.

At LA International, they were met by a hoverlimo that drew admiring glances from the members of the public who saw it, but Bond Team didn't seem to notice. There were drinks, nibbles, and a satellite videovision available in the limo, but the food went untouched and the videovision stayed switched off.

They were checked in to the plushest suites in the finest hotel in the city where the other guests stared: *Who were these four young people who were greeted like royalty, and why did they look so stern?* Their rooms included the services of a virtual butler. They dismissed him on his first appearance, made no comment on the luxurious furnishings and the marble bathrooms, like something a Roman emperor might have coveted, no comment on the breathtaking views of Uptown LA that their accommodation commanded, no comment at all.

To anybody else, the last six hours would have been a fantasy come true, a dream of wealth realized, but to Bond Team, they were nothing. To anybody else, this could have qualified as the beginning of the greatest vacation of their lives, but to Bond Team, their reasons for traveling to Los Angeles were as far from recreational as the Earth from the Sun.

Tomorrow was Jennifer's funeral.

He knew he'd have to eventually, but Jake didn't want to see them. Partly it was because he wouldn't know what to say, or how to act. But then, who did at moments like this — the moments you dread all your life and would do anything to avoid or to bypass but which come knocking on your door regardless, dressed in black, and change your life forever? Partly it was because, sitting or lying or sometimes kind of rolling on the floor alone, utterly alone, he'd remembered more or less how to stop crying, but when he saw the other and heard their voices, all sympathy and sorrow, and the tears shining in their own eyes like coins of great value, he worried that he'd forget again and plunge back into grief, and that this time he'd drown. But mostly, it was because he knew that when they got there — Lori, Cally, Eddie and Ben — together with himself, they'd make five, and there should be six members in Bond Team, and every time he looked at them, he'd be forced to remember that there was someone missing, and who that someone missing was, and why.

And that she'd never be coming back.

In any event, he supposed it wasn't too bad. After getting in touch with Grant, after informing him of Jennifer's . . . of what had happened, Jake had been told to stay put until Grant could reach him, that the senior tutor would take charge of everything. He pretty much had to, arranging the funeral with Aunt Li and transferring Jake to the hotel where he'd remained ever since, never once venturing outside his suite, existing hollowly in what had seemed endless time before the arrival of his team-mates. Then they were somehow at the door; he knew it was them. Then they were inside the room, and around him, and their arms were around him and, it wasn't too bad after all because they'd known Jennifer, and their grief brought them together, closer together, even him and Ben.

"Do you want to talk about it, Jake? Do you think you can?" Cally massaged his shoulders, felt the muscles tight with tension.

"Sometimes it helps," coaxed Lori. She seemed paler than the others, and she wore a scarf around her neck like a bandage, but Jake did not think to ask why.

All he could do was grimace bitterly. "What is there to say? Jennifer's dead because of me."

"How d'you work that out?" Eddie said in bafflement. "Bit hard on yourself, isn't it?"

"No, Eddie, it's not." As if Eddie Nelligan could understand anything beyond a wisecrack and a pickup line. "I was supposed to be watching out for Jennifer, protecting her, keeping her safe, so what do I do? Where am I when she needs me most, when she's fighting for her life, when maybe she's bleeding and broken and calling out for me . . . ?"

"Jake," urged Lori, "don't do this to yourself."

"Where am I? Getting a nice little Mexican meal for two is where I am. Nowhere is where I am, where I'll always be. I swore I'd help her, stand by her. And I stood by and let her die. Jennifer's dead because of me. End of story. No question. She'd have had a better chance if I'd stayed at Spy High with the rest of you. Should have listened to you, huh, Ben? Then Jen might still be alive."

Ben shook his head. "It's our fault more than it is yours, Jake. You were right to come after Jennifer. And we should have come with you. We should have stood together as a team, fought together as a team. For a while I forgot what's important, and it's not rules and regulations. I won't make the same mistake again, Jake, I promise you."

"Meaning?" Jake challenged.

"Meaning that whatever Grant says or wants, after the funeral, we stay here. We stay here, and we finish what Jennifer started. Whatever it takes."

"It was Talon," Jake said grimly, and the name was poison in his mouth. "Somehow Talon got to Jen. Somehow he lured her into a trap. Well, he's going to regret what he did. If he thinks his troubles are over, he's dead wrong." He glanced darkly at his teammates. Four faces and not a flicker of disagreement on any of them.

Later, though, alone with Lori, his mood changed and he seemed able to forget the desire for revenge, at least for now. The others had returned to their rooms — it was well past midnight — but Lori had opted to stay a little longer. Not even Ben had objected.

"How are you really, Jake?" she probed gently.

"Yeah, good, good. Bearing up. My girlfriend's being buried tomorrow — correction, today — but what the heck, there's plenty more fish in the sea, right?" He paced the room restlessly.

"Jake, how are you really?"

"You know the one about 'any better and I'll shoot myself,' Lori? If you've got a shock blaster handy, I'll give you an example."

Lori shook her head sorrowfully. "You can talk to me, Jake.

You don't have to keep your distance. Talk to me. Tell me how you're feeling."

"You want to know? You really want to know, Lori?" He sat next to her and clasped her hands. "Frightened is how I'm feeling, and you want me to know why? I'll tell you that, too, no extra charge. Because I don't have any photos of Jennifer, not one."

"Photos?"

"Yeah, those things you're supposed to put in albums and look back on and smile? Don't have a single photo of Jennifer and me, not even one of Jennifer by herself, and you know why that's frightening me? What if I forget her? What if I forget what she looks . . . looked . . . like. That'd be a betrayal, wouldn't it? Worse even than not being there."

"But you won't forget, Jake," soothed Lori. "You never forget the people you love. They stay in your memory forever. They live in your dreams."

"Dreams, yeah." Jake smiled wistfully. He looked up at the ceiling as if he could see right through it to the deep night sky beyond. "Dreams'd be good. Do you think, if I went to sleep and if I really concentrated, do you think I could make myself dream of Jen, Lori? I'd like it if I could, if I could maybe see her again, and she could talk to me, and we could be somewhere pretty together, somewhere like the far field at home. That was when I first thought I really had a chance with Jen, did you know that? When the four of us went to my dome."

"I didn't know that, Jake, no." Lori spoke quietly, preferring to let Jake just talk.

"Yeah, that'd be a dream worth having. Me and Jennifer and nobody else and the field going on forever. Only if I ever did have it, I'd never want to wake up, but I suppose I'd have to, wouldn't I? Dreams have to come to an end sometime."

Lori squeezed Jake's hands.

"Lori, what am I going to do without her?"

"I don't know, Jake."

He hung his head and sobbed. She held him closer to her.

"I can't go today, to the funeral. I can't do it."

"You can do it. You have to go, Jake. You've got to say good-bye."

"They'll be putting her in the ground. She's in her coffin now, Lori, and she must be so cold and lonely in there, and there's nothing I can do. . . ."

She hushed him tenderly. "Don't think about it, Jake. Remember Jennifer alive. She'd want you to think of her alive."

"But how will I get through it, Lori?"

"You'll find a way, Jake. And I'll be there. We'll all be there. You're not going to have to face this alone."

"You'll be there," Jake said thoughtfully. "I'm glad."

But it wasn't easy.

Jake dressed in the black suit that had been sent for him from Spy High, tailored to his specific measurements and stored in a communal wardrobe for just such an occasion as this. At Deveraux, they hoped for triumph but prepared for tragedy. Black suit. Black shoes. Black tie. Black spirits. And what the heck did it matter what he wore today of all days? He was going to a funeral, not a fashion parade for the bereaved. But when the others, even Grant, appeared in similar mourning, Jake realized why it mattered. Respect. It was part of the ritual, part of the unreality of Jennifer's passing.

The journey to the cemetery was the same. The hearse in front, huge somehow, larger than life, and Jennifer inside, boxed like a gift for God. He and Lori and the others in the car behind, as black as despair. Gazing absently out of the window, he saw people going about their normal business, and people laughing to one another and talking loudly, and all of them oblivious to the hearse's presence and what it meant. Only a small child pointed questioningly at the cars; her mother pulled her arm down and turned her face away. Too young to look at death.

And so, to the cemetery, the muffled sound of car doors closing and the coffin heaved out like luggage. A bright sun. A cloudless sky. *It should be raining,* Jake thought. *There should be grief in the sky and grayness over the world like dirt.* The day was hot, but Jake didn't feel it. A chill that had nothing to do with temperature was in his bones.

And so, to the graveside, on wavering, unsteady feet, and it was a pretty place really, to spend the rest of your death, solemn yet tranquil, the white marble of the headstones and the lush green of the living grass. Jennifer was to be laid next to her family. They'd waited for her, and now their wait was over. It was kind of a reunion.

Jennifer Chen had come home.

He wished that he was blind, blind so he wouldn't have to watch the polished coffin lowered into the ground. He wished that he was deaf, deaf so he wouldn't have to hear the priest intoning the final words that would reach Jennifer's ears before the earth was heaped on. He wished that he was falling, falling into oblivion, but someone was gripping his hand and keeping him standing and it was Lori.

He was nearly alone, though. They weren't exactly lining up at the cemetery gate. Bond Team was there, of course, and Grant, but not Deveraux. No doubt preserving his notorious reclusiveness was far more important than attending the funeral of one of his students. Of Jennifer's family, there was a sole representative. They'd had to lie to Aunt Li, tell her that Jennifer had been killed in a routine mugging. The woman accepted fiction as fact without reservation: She knew what Undertown was like. Aunt Li was weeping into a large silk handkerchief that she'd bought yesterday on sale.

Of Jennifer's other friends, no sign. No Kim. A small, suspicious part of Jake, the part that had not been numbed by the funeral, was surprised by that. It reflected back on Jake's limited knowledge of Kim Tang. And then it wasn't surprised. Then it knew.

Lori felt Jake squeeze her hand in what she interpreted as sudden anguish. "It's all right," she whispered. "I'm here."

But Jake wasn't. He was back in Jen's forlorn apartment, and Jennifer was there, too, and so was Kim Tang. And it was after their raid on the Serpents' drug shipment and Kim was warning Jennifer that Talon wasn't simply going to forget what happened . . . Talon wasn't simply . . . *Talon.* That was it. That was the clue he'd failed to recognize at the time, though he'd sensed that something had been wrong. Talon's name.

Neither he nor Jennifer had told Kim what it was. And Kim had earlier denied to know anything of a guy with scales. She'd lied. And that wasn't the worst part.

Now Jake had a better idea of how Jennifer had fallen prey to Talon.

Jennifer had trusted her childhood friend, and that trust had put her in a box.

A box which had vanished now, becoming one with the deep, dark shadows of the earth. And the service for Jennifer Chen was over, and all her troubles, her anger and hurt, and all her love, too, they were finished with and put away, and a light breeze rippled through the grass.

Time to move on.

When Jake got out of these clothes, he and Kim Tang were going to have words.

The day after the funeral, Senior Tutor Elmore Grant gathered the five members of Bond Team in his suite. He could tell from their drawn and desolate faces that they were still suffering.

"It's been a painful few days," he said, "a difficult time for us all. Loss is always hard to bear, particularly when it's someone on your own team." He sighed and ran his hands through his graying hair. "I selected Jennifer for Deveraux in the first place. It was my decision, so her death is at least partly my responsibility."

"She'd have gone after Talon sooner or later, sir," said Jake, "even if she'd never left Undertown. At least her training gave her a chance."

"Well, thank you, Jake." Grant appreciated the grieving boy's words. "And I suppose I'd better say, for what it's worth, you still have a place at Deveraux if you want it. Yes, leaving the school without permission normally means expulsion, but what's happened with Jennifer changes all that. No sanctions will be applied to anyone for any part of this tragedy, not even for hacking into the school's personnel files." *So they did know,* Ben registered, not that it seemed very important now.

Grant's hair was looking grayer than usual it seemed to Lori, like he was aging before her eyes. "Which means," he continued, "that you can all travel back to school with me if you want to. . . ."

"If we want to?" Jake was suddenly alert, sensing a more vengeful option.

"Or," said Grant, "you can avail yourself of a few days' worth of vacation. Mr. Deveraux thinks you need a break, some recovery time to come to terms with, well, Jennifer's death. I happen to agree with him."

"And where does Mr. Deveraux recommend we spend these few days of vacation, sir?" Ben had seen the cold glitter in Jake's eye.

"Wherever you like. You could even stay here —" Grant paused meaningfully — "if you like."

"I think I will, sir," said Jake. "There's some unfinished business I'd like to take care of before I come back to Spy High."

"Me too, sir." Lori stepped forward, joining Jake. "Maybe I can help Jake out."

"Make it three," Cally added. She looked to Eddie.

"Absolutely," he said. "You know what they say about many hands and light work."

"Ben?" Lori turned to her boyfriend.

"I said I won't make the same mistake again, and I meant it. From now on, Bond Team really does look after its own. I'm in."

Grant seemed pleased, though cautious of showing it. "You're all still first-year students, of course, so officially the rules don't permit you to undertake operations. However, I think for the duration of your vacation we can interpret the rules — how shall we put it? — liberally."

"That's very well put, sir," said Cally.

"And I don't want to know what Jake's 'unfinished business' is, either. It's not relevant." Grant regarded his charges levelly. "But I've got something that just might help. . . ."

PART
TWO

CHAPTER NINE

After dark, and no street lights working. A victim (usually a girl). A stalker (usually a man). An alley (always blind). A cliché, but no less frightening if you happen to be cast in the first of the roles.

The girl was panting, gasping. Poor diet doesn't make good runners. Her chosen escape route had turned out to be a dead end, blocked by an unreasonably solid brick wall. No way out. The wheezes became whimpers as her desperate eyes rolled from side to side as if eager to vacate her face. Her pursuer blocked the alley like a barred gate. He flourished a knife like the conductor of an orchestra.

The man grinned. In the darkness, he could take his time. Stupid girl out alone, should have known better. She deserved what was coming to her. And she could scream all she wanted, give her lungs a real workout. This was Undertown. No one was going to hear her, and even if they did, no one was going to care.

"Someone help me," begged the girl.

And the air trembled, shivered, like it was suddenly feeling the cold.

The mugger let out a cry, sudden, shocked, as his right arm seemed to freeze, as he struggled to move it but failed, as a pain jolted through it, and his fingers were forced to open, and his knife dropped to the floor. His eyes widened in fear as his right arm stretched out toward the alley wall. He tried to grasp it with his left but abruptly seemed to lose control of that limb as well, having it extended by its own volition in the opposite direction. The man wailed in horror.

His intended victim could have darted past him now, but the bizarreness of his predicament entranced her. She looked on openmouthed.

"Stop it!" he cried. "What are you doing to me?"

The girl shook her head to deny responsibility for whatever it was that was happening.

He doubled over, coughing, spluttering, as if seized by spontaneous stomach cramps. Then his head snapped back with the crack of a pistol firing. Blood decided for no apparent reason to spurt from his nose.

The mugger threw himself against one side of the alley. Then he threw himself against the other. Then at the ground hard, like he meant it.

Just as suddenly as he'd seemed to lose control over his body, he appeared to regain it. He swore loudly, scrambled to his feet. The girl thought he might come for her again, but he didn't. Without even glancing at her, he ran, fled the alleyway faster than he'd chased her in the first place, even left his knife behind.

The knife which suddenly floated upright into the air, hovered waist high, as if awaiting further instructions.

The night air trembled again, rippled like dark water. From out of it materialized the cold but handsome features of a teen-aged boy with blond hair, like the bust of someone long dead. "Are you all right?" the face asked politely.

The girl's screams suggested perhaps not, but as she hurtled from the alley before any further inquiry could be made, it was a little difficult to tell.

"Maybe if you smiled, you'd get a more positive reaction," suggested Lori's voice from out of nowhere.

Ben didn't think so. "It's not me. It's the controls of this thing. It seems to be having trouble deactivating itself. No, wait, I think I've got it." A shock suit shimmered into view beneath Ben's head. His body gradually filled in like a hastily executed painting.

"Grant did say the SPIEs were experimental prototypes," Lori reminded him, as she also took solid and shock-suited form in the alley. "If only they were a little lighter on the arm." She examined her left forearm. It was encased from elbow to wrist in what seemed to be a metal cast inlaid with panels and dials.

Ben was wearing an identical device on his forearm. "I guess they weren't designed as fashion accessories," he said. "Surveillance and Protection Invisibility Emitters. SPIEs. No need to be pretty if they do their job."

"S'pose not." Lori squinted into the alley's darkness. "And they do their job, all right. Now that we're visible again, I can't see Jake. Jake?" A knife with a life of its own waved at her. "Oh, there you are."

"Yes, here I am." Jake's familiar tangle of black hair quivered into appearance, the rest of him not far behind.

"All SPIEs together. Though the day I need to rely on an invisibility emitter to take out a mugger is the day I give up Spy High and go back to my pa's farm."

"It's not a matter of reliance," said Ben. "It's trying out the equipment in the field, and we all know what the advantages can be of not being seen."

"I guess," Jake acknowledged grudgingly. His dark mood in reality had little to do with SPIEs. He made a fist. "And maybe it was worth it to see the look on the guy's face when he was getting pounded out of thin air."

"It's just as well we don't have an emitter for Eddie," Lori noted. "No girl would be safe in the shower if Eddie had one of these on his arm."

Jake almost managed a bleak smile. "Didn't seem too pleased about it, either, did he, having to stay back at the hotel. Come to think of it, neither did Cal."

"I explained all that." Ben grew momentarily testy. "Two strategies. Front door. Back door. One of the Serpents might actually recognize you, Jake, so there's no way you can go undercover. And it just seemed to me that Cally and Eddie'll have a better chance of blending in with gang culture than me or Lori."

"You mean Cally and Eddie look more like criminals," Jake said.

"No, that's not what I mean," Ben bristled.

"So you mean you and Lori look less like criminals. Blonds are good. Dreadlocks and red hair are bad."

"You're twisting my words, Jake, and whatever's happened, nothing gives you the right to —"

"Oh, stop it, both of you," Lori snapped. "I thought you'd have grown out of this ridiculous sniping and backbiting by now. We've got more important things to worry about than who should do what on this mission. We've all got jobs to do, and they're all as vital as every one of us, but unless you . . . unless . . ."

Lori felt for her throat. Her eyes closed as in sudden sleep. She swayed on unstable legs, and if Ben hadn't caught her and steadied her, she might have fallen. "Lori! Lo!" Both boys voiced their concern.

"It's all right. I'm all right." Lori waved their attention away. "Just a bit tired, I think. All this stress after . . ." She probed again at her throat. Jake saw the faint and quickly healing pink marks of Sandon's teeth on her skin. He'd learned now what had occurred at the Stoker Institute and was ashamed that he hadn't asked earlier about Lori's recent tendency to wear a scarf. Too consumed by his own self-pity to notice. Well, that would change. "I am better," Lori claimed. "I don't need special treatment. I'm still a member of Bond Team."

"Of course you are," said Ben. "Nobody's thinking otherwise. But let's get you back to the hotel, anyway. Nothing more to do here. The SPIEs work."

"Ben's right," agreed Jake, sounding serious. "Let Eddie know what he's been missing."

"Okay. Yeah," Lori consented. "Maybe I could do with a little rest."

"Goes for all of us," said Ben. "Because tomorrow we make our move for real."

Eddie stood in front of the wardrobe mirror and shimmied a little from side to side. "What do you think? Jimmy Cagney." He suddenly adopted a high-pitched nasal tone of voice. "You dirty rat. You killed my brother."

"What a pity he stopped there," muttered Cally from a chair.

"Um no, don't have the underlying sense of menace quite right on that one." He shuffled some more. "More like a gangster in need of a toilet. What about Humphrey Bogart?" Laconic nodding of the head, slurred speech from one corner of his mouth. "Here's looking at you, kid. Of all the bars in all the streets in all the whatever you hadda walk into . . ." A better idea seemed to occur to him. "Or Marlon Brando in *The Godfather*."

Puffed-out cheeks like an overweight hamster, steepled fingers like a church tower. "I'm not an evil man. I'm gonna make you Serpents an offer you can't refuse."

"Eddie, is there a point to this?" Cally looked out of the window at the sky, darkening now apart from the technicolor bursts of advids. By the time they reached Undertown, the darkness would be total. "We need to be getting along."

"Hold on, Cal. I think Brando's the one." He tugged at his lips. "All I need is some cotton wool to shove in here . . . you got any cotton wool, Cally?"

"Grab some from where your brains should be," Cally complained, "and who are these guys, anyway? Marlon who? Godfather what?"

"Cal," Eddie tutted, "your knowledge of twentieth-century film icons is disappointingly limited. Cagney, Bogart, Brando — some of the finest actors ever to put the gang into gangster."

Cally snorted, "And the point is?"

"Thought I might incorporate some of their mannerisms into my own repertoire for tonight. If we're gonna be infiltrating the Serpents' gang, I think we really need to look and act the part."

"Eddie," warned Cally wearily, "if you venture within a mile of the Serpents with your 'dirty rat' and your 'offer they can't refuse,' the only place you'll end up infiltrating is the morgue, and while normally that wouldn't bother me, all the while we're working as a team, I'd like to think I've got some chance of pulling this mission off. Now it's only a suggestion, but how about we just keep to the cover story, yeah? For Jennifer's sake?"

Eddie winced. *A little unnecessary for Cal to mention Jennifer,* he thought, *a little unfair.* He'd only been trying to lighten the mood.

But "You're right, Cally. Sorry," he said, hanging his head like a puppy in disgrace.

Cally now winced in turn. *Shouldn't have mentioned Jen,* she thought, *a cheap shot when Eddie was just being Eddie. He'd probably only been trying to lighten the mood.* So "No, it's all right, Ed. My fault," she said. "I'm just a bit tense, is all. Ben, Jake, and Lori are already off trailing Jennifer's friend with their SPIEs, I mean, doing something positive, and we just seem to have sat around all day accomplishing precisely nothing."

"Then maybe it's time we make that right," Eddie said. "Does Grant's allowance afford a cab to Undertown? Otherwise," he grinned and puffed out his cheeks again, "I'm gonna have to make the cabbie an offer he can't refuse."

Lori remembered some of the words she'd had to sing in prayers back when her family took her to church: "Immortal, invisible, God only wise. In light inaccessible hid from our eyes." With the SPIE on, she was beginning to understand what the lyrics meant.

Grant had given them a brief spiel about the scientific process involved in invisibility emission; basically, it was something to do with refraction of light. What it meant was that the physical experience of being invisible was like wading through deep water, the light of the world rippling past her in flecks of color, like schools of tropical fish. Her SPIE's setting was such that she could see Ben and Jake alongside her, but they seemed like ghosts, like dreams, and the visible world, too, seemed distant, remote, somehow less important. Lori felt beyond its troubles and its trials, immune to torment and pain. If you couldn't be seen, you couldn't be hurt. Maybe if Jennifer had been equipped with a SPIE, the outcome of her hunt for Talon might have been different. But it was no good dwelling on what might have been. In any case, betrayal might still have undone Jennifer.

And the traitor was just ahead.

To begin with, Lori had thought that the emitters might not be working properly. The way Kim Tang kept snapping her head around, the wide terror in her eyes, it was as if she knew she was being followed and dreaded being caught. But her gaze never locked onto Lori or either of her companions. She couldn't see them. Maybe it wasn't people pursuing her at all that she feared, but guilt and shame and regret, emotions that she was never going to be able to outwalk. She seemed to be wandering randomly, restlessly, pacing the dark streets under the flickering moon for no purpose other than to keep moving. And she smoked relentlessly, as if contracting lung cancer at the earliest opportunity might be one way of bringing her problems to an end.

Unfortunately for Kim Tang, her problems got to her first.

They seemed to appear from nowhere, almost as if they'd been invisible themselves, emerging stealthily from the shadows and surrounding her before she could change direction. Too late to change direction now. Thugs. Serpents. Jake nodded grimly to the others. He recognized among them not only Lee but the man with dark glasses who'd been at the pier and escaped with Talon. Must be someone high up in the Serpents' organization, someone Jake was going to take great pleasure in bringing down.

"Yo, Kim," the man greeted, standing directly in her way. "Where you going in such a hurry?"

"N-nowhere," Kim stuttered defensively. "Uh, hi, Riefer. Hi." Pathetic smile. Gulp. "What brings you down here?"

"Oh, I've got a bit of business to take care of." The man called Riefer made it sound like a threat. "Thanks. Don't mind if I do." He plucked the cigarette from Kim's awkward fingers and took a drag from it himself, making no sign of returning it.

"That's fine," said Kim. "Help yourself."

Ben saw Jake's fists clench and fury cloud his eyes. Couldn't allow it to cloud his judgment, too. He squeezed Jake's shoulders restrainingly. Watch and wait. Use the advantage of invisibility. See if anything here was likely to bring them to Talon.

"Lucky we ran into you, actually, Kimmy," Riefer observed, though the sentiment didn't appear to be mutual. "This bit of business, see, you're kind of involved. Actually, Kimmy, you're kind of it."

"Me?" Kim's desolation was tangible.

"Yeah you, and that interfering friend of yours. You know, the good-looking one, the one who's not interfering anymore. And not so good-looking now, either."

The circle of Serpents chuckled at Riefer's excellent sense of humor. Kim seemed to crumple. Lori had to join Ben in preventing Jake from launching himself on Riefer. There was almost a scuffle. Lee, turning slightly and frowning, almost heard it. That was enough for Jake to calm himself.

"Well, now we're looking for her friend. He's kind of a loose end, and you know how Talon doesn't like any loose ends left hanging. You never know when they might come back to haunt you. So Talon wants him dealt with before we tackle the Wallachians head-on, and as we all know, what Talon wants, Talon gets."

Kim shuddered, shook her head emphatically, twice. "I can't . . . he's not . . . he's gone away. Too late, Riefer. Jake's left Undertown. There's no need to . . . he won't be a problem for you anymore. Trust me."

Curious, Lori thought, and unsettling. Here were Kim and Riefer discussing Jake, and here was the object of their conversation only inches away, unseen and clearly straining with every fiber to tear into Riefer and the other Serpents. But Jake's training held sway. He kept his discipline.

"Trust you, Kimmy?" Riefer found the concept amusing. "Like your friend trusted you?" His hand shot out and seized her.

"Riefer, please," Kim whined. "There's no need for this. I'm on your side."

"Well, I'm hoping so, Kimmy, I'm hoping so." Riefer seemed uncertain. "You certainly proved your loyalty when you brought the girl to us, but then again, you didn't manage her boyfriend, and now you don't seem to be being too helpful. That kind of worries me, Kimmy, and I think Talon'll feel the same."

"No, it's fine. I'll find Jake." Kim was nodding her head as vigorously as was possible with a hand clasped just below the chin. "I'll bring him to you. Trust me, Riefer. Just like Jennifer."

"Well, that'll do nicely, Kimmy." Riefer patted her face with artificial affection. "I told Talon he needn't have any concerns about your loyalty, but you know what he's like. So make it soon, Kimmy, before I have to come looking for you again. And if I were you, I'd cut down on the smoking."

A car pulled up alongside, and Riefer and the other Serpents got in. Kim Tang watched it drive off. Her lower lip was trembling, but she didn't cry, not until the car was well out of sight. Then she did. Then she dropped to her knees on the filthy sidewalk and sobbed. Observing Kim Tang's private agony like she was viewing a film, Lori felt pity for the girl who had led Jennifer to her death, pity and a desire to reach out her spectral arms and comfort her. She turned to the boys to see if they felt the same.

Not Jake. It made Lori gasp. Definitely not Jake. His expression was an unforgiving as the grave.

It was ironic, Cally sighed inwardly. When Grant had first visited and offered her a place at Spy High, she'd agreed to leave her old life behind her, to make something of herself, to work for a better future. Now, here she was, a trainee secret agent and computer maestro, back in a world of poverty and despair, of cold alleys and frosty glances, of sleeping rough and being nobody. And Ben had handpicked her for the role. Was it because she was black? Because she had dreadlocks? Was that where Benjamin T. Stanton Jr. thought she really belonged? Cally frowned. It seemed as if you could never truly escape your past. It clung to you like skin. And if you weren't careful, it could destroy you, like it had destroyed Jennifer.

But maybe Ben was partly right. She would blend in with the losers of the social lottery, because, unlike Bond Team's leader, she understood something about them. She knew why homeless and rejected young people turned to drugs, turned to gangs to find meaning and purpose and a sense of belonging in their brief, hard lives. Because they weren't offered these things from any other source, that was why. Because society didn't value them or provide them with hope, and everybody needed to be valued, everyone needed hope. The existence of full-time psychos like Sandon at the Stoker Institute hadn't altered that essential truth, not in her mind, anyway. Rich kids like Ben and even Lori simply didn't comprehend the realities of life for so many, the forgotten multitudes swarming beneath a sky of glorious advids and a technoworld that, in reaching for the stars, was in danger of losing touch with the earth.

So Cally's lips were set in a thin line of determination. Ultimately, she didn't care what task Ben wanted her to undertake, as long as it was geared to smashing the Serpents. Gangs like them, drugs like Drac, the hope with which they tempted the vulnerable was false, delusional, destructive. Cally was proud to be a part of its defeat. It didn't matter that for now she wasn't fighting megarich maniacs on the edge of space. She was still helping to save the world, from the street level up.

"Looks like we've arrived, Cal." Eddie's words disturbed her reverie. She seemed to register their surroundings for the first time. Their cabbie had been reluctant to drive into Undertown, so they'd got out and walked into its derelict heart. The music they heard now from the building ahead of them, the dull throb of the bass, could have been its heartbeat. "The Cobra Club," said Eddie. "Serpent central, at least according to those reports we monitored."

"You know they're right, Eddie," said Cally. "Besides, they took my call earlier, didn't they? That Riefer guy knew Frankie Gallo. Not getting cold feet, are you?"

"Maybe." Eddie stamped up and down on the sidewalk. "Maybe they'll warm up inside."

There was some activity at the doors, a few bedraggled street kids lining up for admission as if they were in a soup kitchen. The hologram of a rattling and striking cobra that guarded the entry hadn't put everyone off, only those with sense. A single bouncer waited outside ready to keep order.

"Are you dancing?" Eddie asked Cally.

"Are you asking?"

"I'm asking."

"I'm dancing."

They joined the woeful trail of Undertown clubbers. They got as far as the doors.

"Hold it right there," growled the bouncer. "Where do you kids think you're going?"

"Inside, I think," beamed Eddie helpfully. "Are we, Cal? Yep. Inside. Why? Are you gonna escort us to a booth?"

The bouncer's head, bald, hard, and unfeasibly round, like a bowling ball with extra holes, wobbled precariously on his shoulders. It seemed the man had been born without a neck. The movement meant he was laughing. "Go on. Get lost. Before I escort my fist into your smart mouth."

"Don't tell me," grinned Eddie. "You're the current holder of the Cobra Club's Employee of the Month Award. Congratulations. Can we go in now?"

The bouncer's good humor was clearly only temporary. "I told you kids once, and once is all you get. If you're still here in five seconds . . ."

"You can count to five?" Eddie was delighted. "I thought only three."

"Right, wiseguy, that's it!"

It certainly was. As the bouncer clutched for Eddie, the boy stepped quickly to one side, took hold of the big man's sleeve, and pulled. Elementary judo. They'd done it in the first month of class. Use a larger opponent's weight against him. Eddie's move was fluent and economical. The bouncer had a lot of weight. It shuddered onto the sidewalk like a jelly that no one would eat.

"Thanks for your time," said Eddie. "Cally, shall we?"

"You're such a showman, Eddie," grinned Cally as they entered the club.

"Then let's just hope the right people get to hear about us." As a car pulled up unnoticed by either of them.

The motif of seediness about the outside of the club was tastelessly extended to its interior decoration as well. Smoke hung in the stale air like apathy. It was probably a blessing that the lighting was what might be described as dim, though a total blackout might have been even more preferable.

Eddie wrinkled his freckled nose in disgust. "Let's hope we draw the attention of somebody Serpent soon, Cal," he said. "I don't know how long I'll be able to stand it in here."

"Not gonna be a problem, Eddie," Cally replied, indicating the way they'd come. "Looks like Fat Boy's got a family."

The bruised bouncer had somehow hauled himself to his feet and was now waddling angrily toward Cally and Eddie. He was accompanied by two copies of himself. They looked like they meant business.

Eddie wheeled to confront them. "Sorry, guys, I'm just not your type. Find someone else to dance with. What about you, Cal?"

"I doubt they'll be able to keep up with me," said Cally.

The first bouncer managed something like, "You damn kids." Then all three lunged.

They were in slow motion compared to the Bond Teamers.

Strength was never a match for speed. Eddie jabbed out with a foot and the first bouncer went flying, though not very far. *"Why does the word 'Timber!' keep occurring to me?"* he wondered.

Cally was slithering between the other two bouncers like an eel, evading their grasping with ease and identifying their weak spots as she taunted them. Ears were always vulnerable. As one opponent lurched forward, Cally clapped both hands hard against the sides of his shaven head. The man yelled and tottered, permitting a flurry of blows at other key pressure points. Down he thudded.

"Watch out, Cal!" Eddie warned. The third bouncer was behind her. She had forgotten him. A perfectly executed whirl and kick, and he joined his friend on the floor. Eddie laughed, applauded, sensed the return of his own foe just in time. Or maybe not quite. The bouncer's wild swing caught him on the arm Eddie had instinctively raised as a block. The power of even that slightest of blows rocked him, sent him staggering back a few paces. But Eddie was grinning, untroubled. "So you want to get serious, do you?"

"Oh, I think so." The muzzle of a shock blaster pressed against Eddie's temple. "Don't even think of moving," said the man called Riefer.

CHAPTER TEN

"So, you're Eddie and Cally?" Riefer led the two Bond Teamers into a grim little office at the back of the Cobra Club. With its scuffed desk and split leather chair, it looked like it had recently survived an armed assault, and then only just. A pair of Serpent thugs kept up the rear, perhaps to dissuade the teenagers from making a detour. Riefer eased into the swivel chair behind the desk. "And this is how you go about asking for work, is it? Flattening three of my best bouncers?"

"We didn't think sending you our report cards would be much of a recommendation, Mr. Riefer," said Eddie. He and Cally stood in front of the desk, like they'd been summoned to explain themselves in the principal's office.

Riefer laughed. Even though the light in the office was yellowed and dim, he made no attempt to remove his dark glasses. It was as if they were grafted onto his eyes. "Well, Frankie Gallo speaks highly of you, and that's recommendation enough for me."

Cally fought to repress a smirk. Sure, Frankie Gallo spoke highly of them, largely because the voice Riefer had heard allegedly calling from New York City earlier in the day had not in fact belonged to Gallo at all. It had been hers, digitally transformed by the miracle of modern vocal modeling to match the voice pattern of the mobster Frankie Gallo stored on the Spy High database. The real Frankie Gallo remained blissfully unaware of Cally and Eddie's existence.

"How is old Frankie, anyway?"

"He's good," Cally lied. "Told us to say hi."

"Yeah. Good old Frankie." Riefer sighed nostalgically. "You know, Frankie was there when I killed my first man, just to help me out if I did anything wrong. He was generous like that, Frankie was."

"Hasn't changed," said Cally. At least, not according to his file, he hadn't. Cally had come across Gallo while researching Talon. He'd been a onetime Serpent who'd relocated east. The discovery was proving useful.

"Anyway," said Riefer, "Frankie says you two are up and coming stars in his organization but need out of the Big Apple for a while. Drawing a little too much heat, huh?"

"Too much heat?" Eddie repeated. "I've got a permanent case of sunstroke, Mr. Riefer. And all because some kid who was the cousin of the cousin of someone big in the NYPD got in the way of our deliveries, and we had to, well, move him *out* of the way, if you know what I mean."

"So that's what the two of you do for Frankie, is it? Drugs?"

"What else?" Eddie said in apparent bafflement.

"Well, good," approved Riefer. "I think we can do Frankie a favor. Need all the manpower we can get right now. I guess you've heard even back east. These Wallachians pushing their Drac. It's not acceptable, and the time's coming when us and them are going to settle who rules the streets once and for all."

"Just as well we're on the winning side, then," slimed Eddie.

"Right," said Riefer. "That's the kind of attitude that'll get you far. So listen. I like you. You're both young, got a bit of spunk, can look after yourselves. You know the work. It's the youth market that's spending the most, all those kiddies out there craving a little chemically induced excitement."

"We know," said Eddie. "It's a tough job, but somebody's got to do it."

Riefer laughed. "Far as I'm concerned, you're in." He raised his hand to prevent Eddie and Cally's outburst of gratitude. "But mine's not the final say. Talon'll want to talk to you first, and we can't do that until tomorrow. He's a busy man."

Not as busy as he's going to be, vowed Cally darkly. "Tomorrow's good," she said.

"So where are you kids planning on staying?"

"Well actually, it's a plush little alley not far from here," Eddie said. "En suite facilities and everything. Does a great line in three-day-old pizzas."

Riefer nodded. "We can do better than that. Carlo, get 'em some food then take 'em to one of the rooms upstairs. Serpents don't slum it."

"Hey, thanks, Mr. Riefer, sir." Eddie was all wide-eyed appreciation. "That's great, isn't it, Cal?"

"Course, there's only one bed," added Riefer, "but guess that's no problem, right?"

"No," Cally managed through gritted teeth. "That's just great."

"We should have done it then," Jake complained, pacing the hotel room unhappily. The room service meals they'd ordered remained untasted by him.

"What's 'it,' Jake?" Ben said irritatedly. "Done exactly *what* then?"

"I don't know. Something." Jake waved his hands helplessly, exasperatedly. "Whatever it is we're going to do to get Talon. Take this Riefer guy out. Trail their car. Force Kim Tang to —"

"The way I see it, Jake," interrupted Ben, "we may not need to force Kim Tang to do anything."

"Ben's right, Jake." Lori's tone was soothing, sensible. In spite of his anger and frustration, Jake felt himself responding to it. "Kim's in danger herself now. If she doesn't manage to find you, produce you from somewhere, well, I think we know what'll happen to her."

"So the plan is to use Kim Tang rationally," said Ben, "not recklessly, Jake. We use Kim to lead us to Talon, you in full view, me and Lori a little less visible."

"And," suggested Lori thoughtfully, "I think we can afford to trust her now. I mean, tell her what we're up to."

"What?" Jake nearly exploded. "You're kidding, right? Sick joke number one in a series of ten. Collect them all and die laughing."

"I'm not kidding, Jake," Lori said, quietly but firmly. "Didn't you see the way Kim was tonight — after the Serpents left, I mean? Not just scared for herself but hurting. Hurting inside."

"Guilt." Jake seemed unmoved.

"Yes, but guilt means conscience. Guilt means shame and grief, and she knows she's done wrong, the worst kind of wrong you can do, and I think she's suffering, and I think she'd do anything to change the past." Jake grunted skeptically. "And I think she'll help us. Ben?" Lori appealed to her boyfriend.

"You've been taking the psychological profiling seminars seriously, haven't you, Lo?" Ben regarded Lori steadily. "Okay. We'll give Kim Tang a chance."

"Jake?"

"What are you asking me for?" He turned his back like a child having a tantrum. "You want to end up on a slab, you're going the right way about it. But there's two of you, and only one of me. Guess I'm outvoted."

"Don't be like that, Jake." Lori sounded hurt.

"Let's just change the subject," Jake frowned. "Doesn't it worry either of you that Cally and Eddie haven't checked in yet?"

"They'll be all right," Ben said. "Cally knows what she's doing even if Eddie usually doesn't."

Jake refused to be optimistic. "Let's hope so," he said.

Sharing a room with Eddie for the night had been bad enough, particularly on the paltry, single mattress on the floor of the room to which they'd been shown. It was the kind of room where you'd expect to see the remains of dead cats staining the walls. But at least, once left alone together, Cally could be frank and honest with her teammate. At least she could tell him in no uncertain terms that the only undercover activity they'd be indulging in involved deceiving Riefer, and if he thought otherwise, then he was more idiotic than he looked, which would be saying something. At least once Eddie had resigned himself to the special charms of the room's bare floorboards, they could whisper to each other about Jennifer and Talon and how the others might or might not be getting somewhere with Kim Tang.

At least in the room, Cally didn't have to pretend to be a pusher.

But next day it was back to the disguise, back to the role: Serpent wannabe, dealing drugs to babes in arms. She hated it. She hated Riefer, who appeared in the early afternoon with his dark glasses ingrained in position and looking even more loathsome than the previous night. The way he leered at her now, though, the repulsion was clearly not mutual.

"Sleep well, Cally?" he asked, a subtext in his voice.

"Not really."

"Maybe there's some way I can make you more comfortable." An unmistakable hint.

Luckily, a hint was what it remained. Riefer had "a bit of business to take care of," and one thing he did not do was ignore business. "I want you two to come with us," he said. "See how we operate. Let's get in the car."

The vehicle prowled the streets slowly, almost stately, like it had nothing to hide. Cally looked out of the window at the wretched residents of Undertown as they passed. She detected recognition in most of their eyes, recognition of the car itself and of what it meant. In the older people, fear, maybe, and resignation, the acceptance that nothing would ever change for them, and in some, perhaps, the last cooling embers of anger. In the younger people, fear, too, but too often the thrilling, exciting fear of the forbidden, and in some foolish eyes, even worse, envy, desire, a dream that could only end in disaster. Silently, Cally cursed Riefer and others like him for daring to tempt impressionable minds toward destruction.

"Most of the time, this is all we need to do," Riefer was saying from the front seat, "cruise along like this. Mostly our customers come to us. It's like being the Pied Piper in that old story. You know it?" He sighed with nostalgia. "The piper played, and all the children of the city danced to his tune. Thing is, we don't even need music. I'll show you what I mean. Pull up over there, Carlo."

The driver obeyed. Riefer wound his window down and instructed Cally and Eddie in the back to do the same. Cally knew what was going to happen. She knew she wasn't going to be able to stop it, not if their mission objectives were to be achieved.

"Any time now," grinned Riefer, the black lenses of his glasses seeming to wink confidently.

A face appeared at the front window. Another. Boy and girl, not even teenagers from the look of them, maybe related, maybe brother and sister. Despair kept in the family. Cally felt her heart sink and a sickness in her stomach. The children's faces, innocence already marked by addiction, scarred by dependency. The sallow cheeks, the sunken eyes, their hands raised like beggars pleading for scraps. But in one fist, a clump of bills. It wasn't charity the children sought.

Riefer greeted them like old friends. It made Cally want to retch. He was chuckling, reaching out and patting the girl on the cheek, like a magician causing their money to vanish and a little bag of shiny pills, like sweets, to appear in its place. The hopeless, lost smiles disturbed Cally most of all. She could probably cripple Riefer from here. Only a cautionary squeeze of her thigh from Eddie prevented her from finding out for sure.

"Kids, I want to introduce you to somebody," Riefer was saying to his customers, indicating the backseat. "This is Cally, and this here is Eddie."

"Hi, kids," Eddie felt obliged to contribute. "How you doing? Not as well as you will be soon, huh?"

Cally risked the tightest of smiles, said nothing.

"Well, you take a good long look at Cally and Eddie," Riefer advised, "'cause you might well be seeing them again, and if you do, whatever you want, whatever you need to make you happy, they'll be able to help you."

Absolutely not, Cally was vowing. There was a line she would not cross, not for the sake of poor dead Jennifer, not for anyone or anything. Nothing was worth the sacrifice of her principles, not even the mission.

All she wanted was to be brought face to face with Talon. Then the deceptions could be over.

Then all bets would be off.

He didn't have long to wait for Kim Tang to show up, which was just as well. Jennifer's former apartment was an uncomfortable place for Jake to be in now. The good memories, at least those memories that in time might come to be regarded as good, recollections of him and Jennifer together, they were no match at the moment for the bad ones, those that would remain bad and worse than bad for as long as he lived: him calling Jennifer's name and no response, and the cold, sickening realization that something was wrong that could never be put right. He hadn't wanted to return here. What chance was there of Kim Tang appearing? Better to approach her at her own home. But Ben and Lori had insisted, working together for once. Where else would Kim start searching for him? they'd asked. And they were right. And feeling the way he did about the apartment, Jake was almost glad to see her.

The same could scarcely be said of Kim. As she edged nervously into the room, apparently half-magnetized to the wall, not delight but relief and dismay contended for possession of her features. She saw him sitting cross-legged on the floor, didn't think to glance toward the kitchen where Lori and Ben were hiding. "Jake," she said, "it's you."

Jake smiled humorously. "Either me or the winner of the Jake Daly look-a-like competition, West Coast division. How are you, Kim? Haven't seen you since Jennifer was alive."

"No. I . . . I'm sorry. About Jen, I mean. I'm so sorry." She couldn't meet his gaze. Textbook guilt. Even if Jake didn't already know the truth, he'd have been suspecting something by now.

"Thought you might have been at the funeral," Jake pressed. "You know, being Jen's best friend and everything. There was room."

"Yes, I . . . I couldn't make it. But I thought about her, Jake. Believe me, I thought about her."

Jake climbed wearily to his feet. "Is that why you're here, Kim? To think about Jen in the place she lived? If you'd brought some flowers you could have started a little memorial over here somewhere, maybe right on the spot where her parents were murdered."

Kim shifted her weight awkwardly. "Actually, Jake, I came hoping to find you." She seemed to take a deep breath, like a diver about to launch herself from the board. "See, I've got some news. About Jennifer's . . . you know. I thought you'd want to know, I hoped I'd find you before you maybe . . ."

"You know what happened?" Jake advanced on Kim. "Who did it?"

"No, I don't . . ." Kim cringed before him, his blazing eyes. "But I know someone. He's got information. He says he's got information. He won't go to the police, he doesn't trust the police, but he'll tell you, Jake, at least I think he will. If I take you to him. I can take you to him."

"Yeah? Who is he? No, let me guess." Jake held his hands to

the sides of his head. Closed his eyes like a seer. "See, Kim, when I'm not burying my girlfriends, I fancy myself as a bit of a psychic."

"Jake," Kim bleated, "what —?"

"T. The letter T. That comes to mind. T as in Talon. Name ring a bell, Kim? And T as in Tang. And T as in *traitor*. Join the dots, and what have you got?"

"Jake, I don't know . . ."

His eyes snapped open. "T as in Truth, Kim. I want the truth now!" He was shouting. He probably didn't realize it. "Why did you do it? Why did you get Jen killed?"

Kim wailed, a desolate, despairing sound. She slid to the floor, hugging herself for protection.

And then Lori's hand was on Jake's shoulder. "That's enough, Jake."

Kim Tang looked up like a child to the gods. Lori and Ben seemed to tower over her, blond, beautiful, powerful. "Who are you?" she whimpered. "How do you know?"

"We're friends of Jennifer's," said Ben. "This is Lori, I'm Ben. And it doesn't matter how we know. There's just no point in pretending anymore."

Kim shook her head sorrowfully, sobbed from her very heart. "I'm so sorry. I'm so sorry."

"Sorry?" Jake's dark face contorted with contempt. "Yeah, yeah. Not so sorry that you weren't about to lead me into the same trap, eh, Kim? What's the score? You lead me to Talon. I get jumped. You walk out with your conscience clear."

"My conscience isn't clear," cried Kim. "It never will be. It's my fault Jennifer's dead, I know, and I hate myself for it, so much I could tear myself open. But I didn't know he was going to kill her, he said he was just going to teach her a lesson, stop her and you from interfering in the things that didn't concern you. And I said, 'You won't hurt her too bad, she's my friend,' and Talon laughed." She appealed to Jennifer's friends for understanding. "He laughed. And I had to laugh, too. I didn't have any choice. That's why I did it, Jake. I didn't have any choice."

"There's always a choice," Jake said.

Kim denied it. "Not here. Maybe wherever you come from, maybe at that fancy school you go to, but not in Undertown. On these streets, the only choice is live or die, survive or don't survive, and if you want to survive, you side with survivors, who-ever they are." A certain defiance crept into her tone. "Whatever the cost."

"You're a Serpent, aren't you?" Lori realized.

"And you told them about us." Jake completed the jigsaw of the past. "You told Talon it was me and Jen who disrupted their shipment, raided their safehouses. But you and Jen had grown up together. How could you do that?"

"She left." A distant bitterness infected Kim's voice. "She left me for a better life, and I can't blame her. I've never blamed her, but I was left alone with my best friend gone. I was frightened. What could I do? I had to find a way to survive, and that meant doing whatever was necessary. I don't really expect you to un-derstand, Jake, but for many of us, the Serpents aren't just a gang. They're protection. They're family. If we're on their side, they'll look after us. And these days, with the Wallachians muscling in and this new drug Drac —"

"We know about Drac," said Lori, for some reason fingering her throat.

"Yeah? Then you know what a menace it is. Worse than

anything the Serpents deal. Worse than anything Talon could do — or that's what I thought. The Serpents are feuding with the Wallachians, and I thought I needed to help them so I told Talon about you and Jen. Because I was frightened. Because I was alone. Because there was nothing else for me to do."

"But there is now." Lori knelt by Kim. Her pure blue eyes calmed her, steadied her, gave her hope. "You can choose a new side now, Kim. You're not alone. We're here. Help us. Help us get Talon."

"I don't know," Kim moaned. "You don't know what he's capable of."

"He doesn't know what *we're* capable of." The blue eyes steeled. "Jennifer was taken by surprise. We won't be. Stand with us, Kim. Make a choice."

Kim hung her head. "I'm sorry Jake. I was going to betray you, too, but I didn't want to."

"Prove it," said Jake.

Kim raised her eyes to his. There was decision in them, and defiance, and suddenly she looked like Jennifer. "I will," said Kim Tang.

CHAPTER ELEVEN

It hadn't been the most enjoyable day in Cally's life. Dispensing drugs to adolescents on the street and harvesting protection money from terrified Undertown shop owners did not feature prominently on her list of pleasurable ways to pass the time away, but she'd survived them without revealing her revulsions. She and Eddie were still in there pitching for the team. And now as darkness fell, Riefer seemed to think they'd done enough.

"Okay. Funtime over," he announced, expressing a definition of "fun" that seemed somewhat at odds with Cally's own. She was going to have to discuss that with him. Soon. "Time for you to meet the main man. Carlo, the old club."

"Not the Cobra Club?" Eddie complained. "Shame. It's such a great atmosphere there."

Cally felt the tension in her bones increase as they pulled up behind a derelict building that Riefer introduced with strangely misplaced pride. If buildings were buried like people after death, rather than demolished, then this one must recently have been exhumed. Foul smells were in Cally's nostrils as they left the limo. Fear. Hatred. Death itself. A Serpent stench. Talon was inside. She was about to set eyes on the man who'd killed Jennifer. Her palms were sweating.

"Nice place you've got here," said Eddie.

Riefer laughed, his dark glasses twinkling. He led them in. There were grim, bleak corridors and grimmer, bleaker rooms, and the whole place was as black and as secret as a murderer's mind.

Talon was waiting for them.

He was in a room at the end of a corridor that had a desk in it with some ghostly paper scattered, as if to remind itself that it had once been an office. And there were other Serpents present, too, looking like they were ready to audition for one of Eddie's old gangster movies. They encircled Talon like an evil halo. Talon was the center. Talon was the heart.

"So these are our new recruits," he said. "Our potential new recruits."

Cally noted the qualification, knew they had to be careful. Talon regarded them with the reptilian eyes of a snake. He was naked to the waist, and beneath his scales, his muscles bulged and flexed. She felt herself breathing more quickly. Riefer was talking, and Talon was listening.

"Cally. My name's Cally." She must have been asked to introduce herself. Her senses were on autopilot.

"And I'm Eddie." Whose senses were obviously set on auto-bull. Otherwise, he wouldn't be advancing on Talon with his hand generously outstretched like he was about to sell him a set of encyclopedias. "Eddie Nelligan. Pleased to meet you, Mr. Talon, sir, and may I say how picturesque you look today. It puts the butterfly on my bum to shame."

Oh, my God, Cally was dreading. *Don't overdo it, Eddie. You'll get us killed for nothing.*

And Talon's expression was a glower as he regarded Eddie's extended hand, as if the gesture was one of insult rather than introduction. His eyes flickered to Eddie's like a serpent's tongue.

And then he smiled, the way an undertaker must smile upon delivery of fresh clients, Cally thought. And then Riefer smiled. And then, naturally, smiling seemed general throughout the room, and even a smattering of laughter. But Talon still did not take Eddie's hand. They still had to be careful.

"Riefer tells me you work for Frankie Gallo in New York," Talon said. "So if you know Frankie, you'll also be familiar with Paulie Castellano, won't you?"

Eddie was about to cross his fingers and claim that he and Paulie Castellano were like *that*, but Cally got in first with a rather different response.

"Paulie Castellano?" she scoffed. "You're kidding, right? Never heard of him." No such name had appeared in the files. Cally gambled that Talon was testing them.

She gambled right.

"Good," Talon conceded, though his eyes still narrowed. "A trick question. As you obviously now realize. You see, my problem is that I'm fighting a war against a foreign invader, a war I'll win, have no doubt about that, but more than ever, I have to be careful whom I permit to stand with me, even if they come with references from Frankie."

"No problem," said Cally.

"You can't trust anyone these days, can you?" added Eddie.

"I don't," said Talon. "Particularly not when the last time two kids your age turned up out of nowhere, they caused a minor irritation to my operations, and I can't help but wonder at the back of my mind whether your appearance is entirely coincidental."

"We can prove we're on the level, can't we, Cal?" For the first time, Cally noticed, Eddie's fixed grin risked slipping. "Tell us where these other kids are, Mr. Talon, sir. We'll deal with them for you."

"Oh, I doubt that'll be necessary," said Talon. "The first is already dead, and the second will be joining her quite soon."

"Excellent," congratulated Eddie. "Can we watch?"

"Boss." Somebody at the door. If Cally and Eddie had been Jennifer and Jake, they'd have recognized Lee. "He's here. She's bringing him in now."

They managed to exchange glances as the room stirred. Keep bluffing it out, the silent communication went. But be ready for anything.

Talon clapped his hands. "Good. Riefer, bring our young friends along." To Eddie: "Your wish has been granted, it seems." Including Cally now: "You're both going to witness what happens to those who offend me. Follow."

Be ready for anything. Cally thought she was. Until they'd been pushed and shoved through further corridors and out into what had evidently once been the dance floor of the club. Until they'd lined its perimeter and waited in darkness for whatever was about to begin. Until twin shadows entered at the far end and the lights went up, exposing a Chinese-American girl and a boy with black, tangled hair.

Until she saw that the boy was Jake.

"Surprise," said Talon.

Be ready for anything. It was on the first page of the Spy High handbook in big red letters. Like Cally, Jake imagined he knew what it meant. But surely nobody could ever be ready to see two of their teammates virtually standing alongside the man they'd come to kill, as if they belonged to him.

Adapt immediately to changing situations. That was on page two. Cally and Eddie were undercover. They were obviously well on their way to gaining the Serpents' trust. Don't compromise that yet. If plan A failed, it still might be needed.

"Here we go," Jake hissed to Kim Tang. "Be ready to get behind me." His eyes darted to black space on either side of him. "Luck," he addressed the emptiness.

"Surprise," said Talon.

"Not as surprised as you're gonna be, man." From inside his jacket, Jake produced a shock blaster. Didn't waste time. Before the Serpents or Talon himself could react, he fired directly at the scaled man's chest. Kim had told them about the Kevlar armor that was stitched onto Talon's skin. *Stitch this,* Jake thought.

The blast struck Talon square on, staggered him. There was smoke and a blackening patch above his abdomen, but he didn't fall. The shot had failed to penetrate the Kevlar.

"Oh well," Jake muttered, Kim Tang clinging on behind him, "if at first you don't succeed . . ."

But Talon must have been shaken more than physically. "Tang's betrayed us!" He was charging into action, a moving target now. "Kill her! Kill him!" Evading Jake's second shot. Homing in on him like a missile.

But then Talon was colliding with something that wasn't there, something that crackled and sparked. He was thrown into the air, sent crashing to the floor.

The Serpents drew weapons, distracting Jake's attention from his target. Unlike his own weapon theirs were designed to kill. "Keep behind me!" he reminded Kim as he raked his fire along the enemy line. They weren't particularly organized in the first place, but the thugs' discipline was not helped when a sudden spray of shock blasts spat at them from apparently nowhere. The shots were real, though, set to render unconsciousness. They created panic.

Talon was wrestling with thin air on the ground, lashing out as if the very oxygen was his foe, struggling to his feet while his head was cracking backward with the electric force of invisible blows. "What is this madness?" he snorted.

"You men! Idiots!" Riefer was darting forward now, leaving Cally and Eddie alone. "Fire at the source! Fire at the source!"

"It's Lori and Ben," grinned Cally. "But they're still outnumbered. Eddie, what do we do?"

It was a problem. Join forces with their teammates and their cover was blown, but what did that matter now if they had Talon and the entire Serpent hierarchy in their hands? This was it, wasn't it? Mission over. "I don't . . ." Eddie was thinking Spy High handbook page three: *Take nothing for granted.* "Just wait."

"But Eddie . . ."

A lucky shot drew a scream from someone unseen and the air rippled like a lake. A shock-suited Lori rose to the surface grasping an injured arm with the SPIE encasing its lower region shattered.

A second disembodied voice yelled, "Lori!" and it was so close to Talon, it didn't matter that the Serpent could not see its owner for that single moment. He knew where to strike, and did so, hard, more than once.

Ben too shuddered into sight, the sensitive mechanism of his own SPIE broken. Talon swept him to the floor, his shock suit no defense against the ferocity of the attack.

"We'd better wait, Cal," Eddie groaned. It was all going to be over soon.

Several Serpents overpowered Lori, dragged her to the ground and tore off her SPIE without regard to her wound. They were grinning now, confidence rediscovered.

And Riefer was aiming at Jake, lenses trained on him like the sights of a rifle. He squeezed the trigger.

And Kim Tang saw the danger and cried out. She didn't stay behind Jake like he'd told her but sprang forward, into the line of fire, deliberately into the path of the blasts.

And the impact forced the breath from her body and glazed her eyes. And she slumped in Jake's arms, and he eased her to the floor.

Eddie seized Cally's hand. "We're our last hope," he whispered. "Stay cool and wait for a chance."

Cally nodded. Spy High handbook: *Chances always come.*

Kim Tang's eyelids fluttered, and for a moment, she looked so much like Jennifer. Jake sensed the Serpents surrounding him, and he knew he'd failed, just as Jennifer had. Maybe failure was a Bond Team trait. He was numb with it. He wouldn't even feel the pain as a gun was thrust against the back of his head.

Kim was looking up at him. He'd be the last thing she'd ever see, because her eyes were glassing over and there was blood on his fingers. He tried to smile for her. He tried to forgive her. She'd tried to save him, after all. But he found that he didn't care about that. She should have tried to save Jennifer. "I'm sorry . . . sorry . . ." she mouthed. She knew.

She died.

"Your turn now, boy," savored the owner of the gun at Jake's head.

"No. Not yet." Talon's voice crackled with authority. "Bring him over here. His silver-suited companions, too. And don't be too gentle about it."

They weren't. Jake was yanked rudely away from Kim Tang's body and he, Lori, and a scarcely conscious Ben were dragged toward Talon.

"Riefer, attend. Our two new recruits as well." Talon was smiling. It wasn't pretty.

Jake glanced at Lori and Ben. Their shock suits had been damaged along with their SPIEs. They had only their wits to rely on now. Or maybe Cally and Eddie. Ben was shaking his head, trying to clear it. Lori was hurt but not defeated. *Wait for your chance,* Jake repeated in his mind. *Chances always come.*

Eddie tried to regard his captive teammates with nothing more than casual interest, to register not one hint of recognition. The only good part of that was that he got to sneer at Ben. "These more of those kids you were telling us about, Mr. Talon, sir?" He shook his head dismissively. "Don't look like much to me."

Cally tried not to look at her friends at all. Riefer was next to her. His presence made her feel sick.

"Who are you?" Talon addressed himself to Jake, Ben, and Lori. "These electric suits. Invisibility. You can't be working alone. Who's sponsoring you? The Wallachians? Tell me. Who sent you?"

"Jennifer Chen sent us." Jake glared.

Talon chuckled. "Talk or you'll soon be seeing her again."

"Save your breath, snake-man," Ben scorned. "You might need it."

Talon tutted like a teacher when the guilty student won't own up. "Ah, well, I suppose it doesn't matter. You're not important enough for it to matter. Lee. Carlo. Your blasters." He held out both hands and received an obedient gun in each.

Lori found herself hoping that Cally and Eddie had a plan.

Ben conserved his strength. He'd all but recovered from Talon's beating. He was poised to move. Stantons didn't die in derelict old clubs.

Jake thought of Jennifer. It was the thought that would keep him alive.

"You gonna shoot them, then, boss?" Riefer wondered politely.

"Oh no, Riefer, I'm not going to shoot them." Talon sounded almost shocked. "Your two new recruits will." At a gesture, several of the Serpents directed their weapons toward Eddie and Cally. "Just to be on the safe side," Talon explained. "Now Eddie, Cally —" he gave them the guns — "the time has come for you to prove your loyalty. You said you'd deal with the kids for me. Here's your chance. All you have to do is kill them. That's all."

Cally and Eddie stared at each other in barely repressed horror. The guns were heavy in their hands. *Chances always come,* Eddie reminded himself. But what if they didn't? His three friends were struggling uselessly. No time. "But, Mr. Talon, sir . . ."

"Do it."

In a kind of surreal trance, they raised their blasters.

CHAPTER TWELVE

The roof ruptured. There were implosions in a dozen places, fissures ripping through the steel and concrete with deafening and pulverizing power. Debris showered onto the Serpents below. Astonished eyes were automatically raised — even Riefer's, even Talon's.

But not Bond Team's. Chances always come, even if you have no idea where from. You just have to be ready to take them.

Jake, Ben, and Lori snapped into action. A sweep. A kick. A throw. They were free.

Cally and Eddie diverted their aim swiftly. Talon's ribs were a tempting target for Eddie. Cally found a spot right in the middle of Riefer's dark glasses. But neither shot was made.

Gunfire exploded from the roof, sizzling like burning rain, as men in black suits and masks dropped into the club on lines hung from helicopters glimpsed far above. Even Bond Team were shaken momentarily by this new development.

"Wallachians!" cursed Talon, the skin beneath his scales livid with hatred. "Damn them! It has to be!"

With a glance, he absorbed the fact that his Serpents were going to be no match for these well-armed, well-drilled invaders. Already the collapse of the roof and the fusillade of shock blasts had wrecked their ranks with panic and chaos. The likes of Lee were already breaking for it while they still could.

Then his eyes took in Eddie, and the blaster pointing at him — point blank. Even the Kevlar might not protect him at such close range. But Eddie's eyes were on the roof, gazing up at the Wallachians wheeling in the air, creating carnage like a crazed circus act. He should have remembered: *Eliminate your nearest foe first.* Talon knocked the gun from his hand, but Eddie recovered quick enough to duck his second attempted blow.

"You're getting old, pal," he taunted. "Time to put you out of your misery."

"Child," threatened Talon, "I'll break you in half."

But a blistering swathe of shock blasts ripped up the floor between them, divided them. The moment passed, and survival became Talon's priority. Escape. He could settle the score with this boy another day.

The Wallachians were leaping from their lines, bursting in at the door, and the idea of escape was occurring to Ben as well. Lori was with him. They'd both wrested blasters from fallen Serpents. "Let's get out of here." The words were needless. Lori didn't bother assenting. "Where are the others? I can see Eddie. What about Cal?"

The gunfire and explosions around her didn't matter. They were fireworks. They couldn't harm her. Cally darted through them certain of her own invulnerability. What mattered, who mattered, was *"Riefer!"* His name ulcered her mouth. "Riefer! I'm coming for you!"

He was cowering in a corner. Things weren't going according to plan. He saw Cally bounding toward him, knew that he'd been deceived before. He raised his gun to put matters right.

Like quicksilver, Cally ducked low, the blast passing by harmlessly. Then she was slamming into Riefer before he could fire again, disarming him, disabling him. "Not so clever when you're not feeding filth to kiddies, huh, Riefer? Not such a big man when your victims fight back?"

But Riefer wasn't listening. His head lolled back abruptly, and his glasses fell to the floor. His horrified eyes stared, wide and open and the pure, innocent blue of a baby's.

Cally wheeled. The Wallachian who dispatched Riefer was now training his pulse gun on her. She took a deep breath, one that might last her into the afterlife. It was all . . .

"Over for you, Talon!" Jake pursued him through narrow corridors. "You're not getting away from me!" But there was gunfire from behind, raking the walls, the ceiling. And gunfire from ahead, too, shells sparking with impact on Talon's armored skin, raising welts but not slowing him down. He smashed into the Wallachians, threw them aside as if they were weightless, as if they were toys. He snatched up a shock blaster and pivoted.

Jake threw himself to the floor as Talon blazed away at where he'd been. The Wallachians following caught the onslaught instead, and by the time Jake had scrambled to his feet to renew the chase, Talon was gone.

"Not again!" Jake groaned. "Jen, I nearly had him."

But there was no possibility of further pursuit. "Try anything I don't like, and you're dead," promised the heavily accented Wallachian with the shock blaster trained on him.

"Yeah? What don't you like?"

"Kids with smart mouths. Now move!"

Jake was marched back the way he'd come, back into the devastated room of the club. He didn't know what he'd expected to see, but the Serpent bodies on the floor wasn't a good start. Where were the others? Maybe they'd escaped. Maybe they were free. Don't let them be dead. Not like Jennifer. He couldn't bear it if . . .

Jake didn't have to go there. He saw them and breathed a sigh of deep relief. His teammates had been herded into the center of the dance floor. They were alive. As he was marched to join them, he also realized that they were the only prisoners taken. He wondered why.

"Jake, you're all right!" Lori was equally relieved to see him.

"Talon?" Ben asked.

"He got away." The admission was reluctant, like failure.

"For once, I wish we could join him," Eddie said. "Hey, you, yeah, you in the balaclava. You think you could point that blaster somewhere else, huh? It's wreaking havoc with my nerves."

The Wallachians, not unexpectedly, ignored Eddie's demand.

"Maybe we ought to be grateful," Cally suggested. "If these Wallachians hadn't intervened when they did, our situation might have been even worse than it is now."

"Cally's right," said Ben. "We're alive, and we're together. I'd have taken that a few minutes ago."

"You're a real ray of sunshine, Ben, do you know that?" Eddie almost applauded. "For a second there, I nearly forgot we were surrounded by a bunch of masked psychopaths with enough weaponry between them to wipe out a small army, and it's all kind of aimed at us. Just slipped right out of my mind."

"Eddie," Ben retaliated, "you don't have a mind."

"What I want to know," mused Lori, "is if these people are Wallachians, why are they here? And why now? Why just in time to save us?"

"Agreed," nodded Jake, "and it's what's been bothering me. Why *have* we been saved? How do these jokers know we're not Serpents?"

"Questions, questions." A voice from behind them, bullishly good-humored and uttering its words in a thick Eastern European accent. "So many questions." Bond Team turned to see a large, heavily whiskered man walking briskly toward them, flanked by more armed and masked subordinates. "Perhaps you deserve some answers. After all, if not for the five of you, our success tonight might not have been possible."

"Who are you?"

"Great question, Ben," said Eddie. "I'd never have thought of that one."

"You may call me Boris," permitted the heavily whiskered man.

"No kidding. I was hoping for Igor."

Like everybody else, Boris ignored Eddie's quips. "And yes, young lady, Lori, is it not?" She wasn't alone in surprise that the man seemed to know her name. "Yes, Lori, we are Wallachians and proud to be so."

"Seems you know more about us than we do about you," said Ben.

"Of course. We followed you here. We have been watching you for days, since that night when Jake and the late Jennifer Chen disrupted the Serpents' drug delivery at Pier Twenty. We have learned much in that time of your hatred for the man known as Talon. It is a hatred that has kept you alive tonight because it is a hatred we share."

"I suppose it's too much to hope that you picked him up on your way in?" Eddie wondered. "He'd save us all a bit of time."

"I am afraid that Talon has eluded our vengeance," Boris conceded gravely. "For the moment."

"So I guess that means we all go home, then, right?" Eddie perked up. "Any chance of a lift?"

"You are not going home, Eddie." Boris reached into his jacket and produced a handgun of his own. It looked like a shock blaster but wasn't. "None of you are."

"Now wait," Ben calmed. "What do you want with us?"

"I want nothing," Boris said, "but I am the servant of one who wishes to speak with you. All of you. Even him." Indicating Eddie.

"What do you mean, even me?" Eddie protested, offended.

"The shells in my gun are not fatal," the Wallachian continued. "They simply contain a strong sleeping draught. Quite harmless but most effective."

"Boris," edged Cally, "why are you telling us this?"

The whiskered man smiled. "So that you know, when I shoot you, it is not the end."

He fired five times. Didn't miss once.

The worst thing about being knocked senseless in the course of duty, Eddie thought as his mind gradually drifted back toward consciousness, was the possibility of never waking up again at all. But the second worst thing was never knowing, just before you opened your eyes, where you'd be or how long you'd been out of it. He'd fantasized once or twice (okay, actually quite often) about coming to on a bed with white satin sheets and this beautiful girl with not very much on kind of mopping his brow and gazing tenderly at him like she'd got it in mind to kiss him better. That kind of thing might happen to Ben, though, or even to Jake, but never to Eddie Nelligan, guaranteed never. He was more likely to recover and find himself chained to the wall in some retro-medieval torture chamber. So this time, he figured it might be wiser to feign oblivion a little longer and wait for a clue as to whether it was worth letting the world know he was conscious again or not. *Might* be wiser.

But then, Eddie wasn't that clever.

"Hi, Ed. Welcome back."

Okay, so it wasn't his beautiful girl with not very much on, but it was Cally in an evening dress, and that wasn't a bad start. The bed he was lying on had satin sheets, too. "Hey, Cal, you here to mop my brow or what?" he said.

"I luh?"

"Nothing." Eddie sat up and wished he hadn't. A secondary effect of the knockout shell had been to transplant a very loud and very untalented rock band into his head. "Ouch, ouch, ouch."

"Poor baby," Lori sympathized from across the room. She was elegantly robed in blue. "Don't worry, Eddie. The pain wears off in a few minutes."

"A few minutes we might not have." Ben was here, too, all his team leader buttons well and truly pressed. (Eddie had hoped it might be just him and the girls. Wherever here was.) "We need to assess our situation. Eddie, just try and keep up."

"Right. Er . . . you don't have any aspirin, do you?" He made a play of patting at where his pockets should have been. They weren't. Largely because he was no longer wearing the jeans and T-shirt of his previous waking moments, but a tuxedo and bow tie. So were Ben and Jake, who now prowled into view. And both of the girls were in evening dresses. Eddie saw a pattern emerging. "If they'd wanted us to go to a prom, why didn't they just ask?"

"All right. Point one. Clothes." Ben ticked it off. "No sign of our own, and someone's gone to the trouble of dressing us up like star guests at an awards ceremony."

"Or like lambs to the slaughter," said Cally.

"Unlikely," Ben seemed to think. "If they wanted us dead, we'd be dead by now. So why this charade?" He tugged at his perfectly tailored sleeves as if wearing the tuxedo made him physically uncomfortable.

"They've braided new beads into Cally's dreadlocks," Lori noticed. "Looks like they've even combed Jake's hair."

"Correction," Jake pointed out, rubbing his black mop vigorously with both hands. "Tried to. And my theory is they want to make us presentable for someone they think is the main man."

"The guy who wants to 'talk with us,'" Ben concurred. "Boris said he was a servant, so I think we're talking tradition here, hierarchy — obeying orders without question. That might be something we can use. Okay. Point two: the room."

It was impressive, certainly, but like something from another time. The walls were made of great slabs of stone and hung with rich tapestries depicting scenes of hunting on horseback, archery, falconry, and the polite conversations of aristocratic men and women in gardens of gold. Five beds, each gorgeously draped in satin, encircled a great fireplace with a chimney that reached to the arching stone ceiling. No fire was burning. The only concession to twenty-first century tastes seemed to be the adjacent marble bathroom and the light panels set into the ceiling.

"I guess they figured torches would be too easily used as weapons," Lori observed. Plus rugs rested on the flagstoned floor. The door was of unyielding oak and stoutly locked; Jake had already bruised his shoulder discovering just how stoutly. "It's like one of those old European castles from the Middle Ages," she concluded.

"Terrific. Where's Robin Hood when you need him?" Eddie grumbled.

"We can't have been taken to Wallachia, can we?" Cally didn't seem enamoured by the possibility. "I mean, is this supposed to be what's outside?"

A row of windows punctuating one wall seemed to gaze out upon a deep valley with forests and mountains beyond, a scene stolen from a pre-industrial past.

"Well, let me tell you, Cal," volunteered Eddie, "that's not LA."

"It's not Wallachia, either." Jake rapped his knuckles against each apparent window in turn. Metal every time." Viewscenes. Part of the illusion. Someone's on a nostalgia kick, all right, but we could be anywhere."

"So we're dealing with a major league schizophrenic, right?" said Cally. "Doesn't know whether he's living in the past or the present. Not facing up to reality."

Ben nodded. "Then let's not make the same mistake. Our reality is we're prisoners. It doesn't matter where. So, Point three: How do we get out of here?"

"There's the chimney," Lori wondered, feeling up above the fireplace. It was blocked.

"Guess that'd be too easy," Ben considered. "And no real windows. No access to the outside at all."

"What about we call room service and just jump the guy when he comes in?" Eddie warmed to the idea. "One of us can dress up as him, and the others hide under the trolley."

"Do you think Eddie's suffering a latent psychological breakdown after being shot?" Cally asked.

"Listen." Jake waved the trivia away. "The way I see it is this. Why don't we just stay put for a while? This Wallachian Mr. Big wants to talk to us, right? So to do that, he's either got to come to us or summon us to him. Either way, sooner or later that door is going to be opening. And so is our way out of here."

As if in direct response to Jake's words, the grate of bolts being drawn was heard from the other side of the door. "Sounds like it's sooner," Lori approved.

"Right. Everyone on their toes." Ben flexed his limbs like an athlete before a race. "Keep your wits about you."

"Did I pack my wits today?" Eddie asked.

Bond Team came together, forming a line facing the door, Ben in the center flanked by the girls and then Eddie and Jake. "I'll tell you one thing," Jake said. "No one is shooting me again. No one."

But this time, Boris didn't look as if he wanted to. The door opened. The whiskered Wallachian entered with the geniality of a party host, no weapons in either outstretched and welcoming palm. The pair of silent lackeys who accompanied him, however, were a different matter, their guns discreet but visible. All three men were clad in flowing black robes. A heavy gold chain hung around Boris's neck like a signature of office. "The mayor of Wallachia," muttered Eddie.

"Ah, you are ready," Boris smiled broadly. "And how fine you all look."

"Ready for what?" Ben wanted to know. "Where are we? What's —?"

"No, no, no." Boris closed his eyes in pain. "Dinner first. Questions later."

"Dinner?" Eddie echoed. "Hey, Boris, does your chef know I'm on a gluten-free diet?"

"Follow me, please," invited the Wallachian. "Now." To remind everyone that it was not really an invitation at all.

So they followed him, the armed lackeys keeping up the rear, through corridors, which, like their room, were cut from castle stone. Suits of armor stood sentinel in alcoves. Bond Team made a note — there was a ready supply of swords and maces. No tapestries here, though the walls displayed at regular intervals an inexhaustible number of identical flags. Red crosses on white. The flag of Wallachia, Lori remembered from their Threat Analysis session. Boris strode ahead briskly, with the familiarity of someone who knew where he was going. Ben, meanwhile, tried to visualize the route they were taking in his head, to make it a map they could use later to find their way out.

"Are we building up an appetite here or what?" Eddie grumbled. "It'd have been quicker to go to McDonalds."

"We are here," said Boris proudly. More oak doors. Guards to open them. And beyond, a banquet table of polished mahogany set for a feast. The chairs were high-backed, richly carved, like thrones, and only one was occupied. At the far end of the table waited a man who, even though seated, seemed tall, seemed dominating. He wore robes that were similar to those of Boris but decorated, red on black, with a swirling black cloak clasped at his throat. A chain was draped over his shoulders and rings adorned each of his fingers, every piece studded with rubies, all a lustrous crimson, like stones of blood. His hair was as black as his clothing, as was his beard, but his skin was white. Not pale, but white. It stretched tautly across cheekbones that seemed so pronounced, so sharp, that it was a surprise they didn't slice through the flesh to reveal the bare bone beneath. But the eyes, they seemed to have no whites at all, and their color was of deepest night.

Ben worried that he'd seen this man before, not close up, maybe not even his full face, but there was something about him, a presence, that reminded him of . . . what? A successful secret agent had to be able to see connections that others would miss, had to be able to remember everything. He was leader. He was a Stanton. He could do it. . . .

Lori touched him, whispered in his ear. "I think it's Tepesch. The president of Wallachia."

Ben understood, suddenly knew, why they'd been sent to Stoker. Lori had been right all along. Drac was a killer and the Wallachians were pushing it, and in charge of the operation was a very main man indeed, an ultimate Mr. Big. The president himself.

He rose as the small group entered. Tall, like a pillar of darkness, exuding power and purpose.

Boris bowed low. "My prince," he announced, "your guests have arrived."

"Indeed." His voice hovered in the air like a bat. "Approach, young ones. Approach and allow me to introduce myself."

Bond Team obeyed, though reluctantly. Cally felt it was like being beckoned to the gallows. She felt her feet dragging on the smooth flagstones.

"Good. That is good. I am what you Americans would call

the president of my country." Half-smile, half-sneer. "But where I was born, such a concept is strange and alien. Where I come from, power is seized by the strong, not granted by the weak, and I am strong indeed. I am Vlad Tepesch, Prince of Wallachia." He gestured. "Sit, please. Enjoy the meal that is to be served." Lips peeled back like paper, and sharp teeth gleamed. "It could be your last."

CHAPTER THIRTEEN

It wasn't exactly the most fun meal Lori had attended. Their host, the so-called prince of Wallachia, didn't actually touch any food himself, instead he sipped constantly at what looked like the reddest of wines, the crystal goblet constantly replenished by a waiter. The members of Bond Team were hardly wolfing their food down, either. There were other things on their minds than the succession of dishes that were produced for their delectation. In fact, Lori absorbed, only Boris, who had also been invited to dine, was making the most of the opportunity. He was gorging himself with gusto. *Looked like a bull, ate like a pig,* she thought uncharitably from her chair to the man's right. On her right sat Ben, closest to Vlad Tepesch at the head of the table. Cally was opposite her, with Eddie and Jake to her right and left respectively.

"These are all native dishes from my homeland," Vlad Tepesch said.

"Yeah?" Eddie wrinkled his nose. "You get a lot of emigration in your neck of the woods?"

"Is the honest produce of Wallachia not to your liking?" Tepesch feigned surprise. "Perhaps your stomachs would be happier if I supplied them with your own country's culinary staples. Burger, fries, and what is the phrase? A hot dog with everything."

"You'd do that?" Eddie perked up. "Really?"

"No," said the president of Wallachia. "It just amuses me that your food should be as disposable and unsatisfying as every other aspect of your culture."

"You've got something against our culture, Tepesch?" said Ben defensively.

Vlad chuckled coldly. "I have issues. My people have issues. You see, though my true place is *with* my people, I have traveled to your country before, on more occasions than you can imagine, and I have observed."

"Really?" Cally said skeptically. "And what have you observed?"

"A lack of faith." Tepesch warmed to his theme, his black eyes glittering. "A lack of belief in anything beyond hollow consumerism, beyond videophones and holovision and virtual reality entertainment. Your senses are full but your souls are empty, and it is this emptiness, this absence of meaning in your lives, that is the weakness at the heart of your society, the flaw at the core of your century." A ringed and admonishing finger was raised. "Beware, my young friends, for it is lack of belief that your enemies will use to destroy you."

"And are you one of our enemies, President Tepesch?" asked Lori.

Vlad smiled. "If I did not consider there to be a mutual interest between us, Lori Angel, then you would not be breathing now."

"We're listening," said Jake.

"Then let me begin by telling you a little about my homeland. I doubt Wallachia features prominently on your self-serving educational curriculum."

"You'd be surprised," muttered Ben.

"Mine is a small country," Tepesch pursued, "but a proud nation. A land of great beauty, of fertile fields and deep forests, plunging valleys and dancing rivers, a land rich in nature's goodness, encircled by mountain peaks like a crown. My people believe that their birth in Wallachia is not a random accident but a gift of the gods, and that they are bound by ties of honor and blood to protect the traditions of their homeland and to preserve its independence. This belief beats strongly in the hearts of all, from the lowliest peasant to the prince of Wallachia himself. Myself," Tespesch added almost apologetically.

"Do we get to applaud yet?" mumbled Eddie from safe distance.

"That's all very well," Cally said, "but how does safe-guarding your own country square with spreading Drac in ours?"

Tepesch inclined his head slightly. "Perhaps there is one of my ancestors, of whom you may have heard," he said, as if this were a relevant response to Cally's question. "He lived in an earlier time, over half a millennium past, a fiercer yet perhaps more noble time, when the fate of nations was rightly decided on the battlefield and fought out between warriors mighty in the arts of combat."

"My ax is bigger than your ax," Eddie whispered to Cally.

"His name was Vlad Tepesch also, though he came to be known by another name, a title that has since passed into legend. Vlad the Impaler."

Eddie raised his hand. "Excuse me for interrupting, but is that 'impaling' as in, you know, long and rounded metal poles and kind of sticking people on them and kind of just letting them hang there? Is that what we're talking about here?" The president of Wallachia's humorless smile confirmed it. "Nice guy," Eddie finished lamely.

"We may balk these days at the impaler's methods," Tepesch allowed, "but it cannot be disputed that he defended his homeland against all potential invaders — and there were many — with vigor and ruthlessness, and in war he was never vanquished. His is an example that every subsequent ruler of Wallachia has sought to follow, even as sword was replaced by cannon was replaced by musket was replaced by tank. The princes of Wallachia have ever stood firm in their country's defense and ever will do so. It is our purpose. It is our responsibility. None of foreign blood will ever win Wallachia and, until this day, none ever have . . ."

"Excellent news," said Eddie as Tepesch lapsed into thoughtful silence. "I'm happy for you."

"Be quiet, you babbling fool," snapped Boris, "unless you wish your tongue to form part of the next course."

Eddie zipped his lips. "Mm mmmm mm, mm?"

Until this day, Ben was thinking. *So what was happening now to change things? Why was Tepesch flooding the drug market with Drac now, as opposed to last year or next? What had the Threat Analysis said?*

"I am the latest in a line of warriors." Tepesch was speaking again. "I am part of a proud tradition and I will face any foe on the field of battle, man to man. But you Americans, in your sterilized, insulated, consumerist paradise, you have no honor, no pride, no respect. You fight not with arms but with finance. You wage war not with weapons but with computers and codes. Your force is not military but economic." Tepesch sighed, and for a moment, it might even have been possible for Ben to feel a sense of sympathy for the baffled prince. Until he remembered Sandon and Drac and what had nearly happened to Lori. "How can I battle a balance sheet? How can I defeat the dollar?"

"Are these rhetorical questions," Eddie ventured, glancing at Boris, "or are you after some answers?"

Tepesch seemed to recover himself, laughed heartily. "I have the answers, boy," he beamed, "and I intend to share them with you. A new kind of war is being fought today, and the prince of Wallachia is ready. Come. Follow me. Dinner is over."

"Compliments to the chef," muttered Cally, her dessert untouched on the table.

Tepesch strode from the room and Bond Team had to hurry to keep up, Boris and the guards behind them. Lori whispered urgently in Ben's ear: "This is about corpornation status for Wallachia. I'm sure of it."

"I think so, too," Ben whispered back, though he hadn't until now.

Tepesch stopped dead. He turned to Lori, almost in admiration. "You are a clever girl," he said, "and in a way you are correct. The world has globalized, I believe the term is. Small and economically weak countries are at the mercy of financially stronger nations like never before. Indeed, the poor are now the vassals of the rich — a new kind of slavery. So the proud lands of Africa, of Asia, of Eastern Europe are made to grovel to the wealthy West for handouts, for the monetary crumbs from your table. And these crumbs, like pittances, grants, and investments, will be sprinkled on the ground for us to nuzzle like pigs, and all we have to do to earn them is surrender our sovereignty, give up our independence, and be ruled by corporate bankers in skyscrapers half a world away. Become a corpornation? Become the possession of the United States? No, my dear. Not Wallachia."

They were standing by an alcove with a suit of armor in it. Tepesch twisted the suit's gauntlet and the stone wall, which wasn't really stone after all, split open like a smile. Beyond was a glass elevator. Beyond that, acres of modern office space, complete with computer consoles and videolinks. The night-lighting was on, and through distant windows, darkness could be seen. By day, the place was probably thronging with power-dressed executive types, totally attuned to the twenty-first century.

"Talk about culture shock," Jake murmured.

The elevator took them down.

"Your foolish government," Tepesch continued scornfully, "believes that I have entered your country to negotiate my people into economic servitude, to seek this so-called corpornation status. But such is far from the case, as you have no doubt realized."

Then they were still in the states, Ben was bargaining. In fact, given the feud between the Wallachians and the Serpents, they were probably still in LA.

The elevator came to a halt and the group emerged into a laboratory of some sort. Vats of chemical simmered and brewed like technowitchcraft. Tubes and vials bubbled with what Ben instinctively knew was blood. Scientists lovingly monitored whatever process was going on here.

"What is this?" he said distastefully.

"You're manufacturing Drac, aren't you?" Lori realized in horror. "This is where you make the drug."

"A clever girl, indeed," Tepesch chuckled, "and correct again. This is how I will keep Wallachia free from American occupation. I will counter one form of invasion with another. One that is even stealthier, even more insidious. Under your government's nose, here in the inviolate sanctuary of the Wallachian Cultural Exchange Building in Los Angeles, the means of your downfall is being produced. Radescu, bring me the flower."

Eddie looked confused. "What, from drugs to floristry in one swift move?"

One of the scientists, evidently Radescu, scuttled forward and offered up a single cut flower. The bloom's petals were purest white, but the seeds at its heart were the crimson of blood.

"The dracul, or *dragul,* flower," explained Vlad Tepesch. "It is native only to Wallachia, and even there grows nowhere but in the darkest and most inaccessible regions of our forests. Beautiful and delicate, is it not?"

"Very nice," Cally humored.

"Yet in the language of my fathers, 'dracul' means 'devil,' and the flower did not earn its name without reason. The seeds, you see, these scarlet pods, when crushed and consumed, have an effect on a man. They increase his strength, his power, his sense of well-being. They can turn a mighty warrior into an unstoppable force. They can transform a man into a god." Tepesch turned his black gaze from the dracul flower to Bond Team. "Though there are one or two side effects."

"Dracul?" Lori was looking for links. "Dracula?"

"Precisely, Lori," Tepesch said. "The source of the Dracula legends lies with my great ancestor Vlad the Impaler, and the source of the vampire myth itself lies with the innocent beauty of the dracul flower. Vampirism and its lust for blood was never the result of a communicable infection, it was the by-product of a drug."

"So Drac's made from this flower the way heroin comes from the opium poppy," Ben grasped.

"Indeed. And thanks to the wonders of modern biochemistry my scientists have been able to refine the natural process of Drac manufacture. The drug which is being supplied on your streets — at a very competitive price, too, I might add — grants the user an unprecedented euphoria, almost an ecstasy, you might say, but then also increases rather considerably the craving for violence and blood that Drac inevitably brings with it. And, of course, we have made the substance wildly, uncontrollably addictive."

Cally lunged forward suddenly and was only just restrained by Boris. Bond Team flexed to help her but the guards' guns were too many and too near. Now was not the time. Cally didn't seem to care, anyway. "Don't you realize what you're doing?" she spat. "You'll kill thousands, destroy the lives of thousands! Don't you understand?"

"No," Tepesch gloated. "Don't *you* understand? That is precisely my intention. If thousands die, good. If tens of thousands, even better. Only when the streets of America run red with blood, only when the addicts I will have created have brought this nation to its knees will I rest and be still and consider myself fulfilled."

"That's a pretty warped kind of fulfillment," Jake snarled.

"To each his own," chuckled Tepesch. "It's a free country, isn't it?"

"But you won't get your victims," Lori claimed. She remembered the Stoker Institute. Her throat smarted. "Treatments are already being developed. People won't take Drac when they see what it does to them."

Tepesch shook his head almost sadly. "Perhaps not so clever after all. If there are ever treatments, my dear, we can mutate the drug. And as for there being no takers, the first step to addiction is despair, and the first step to despair is having nothing to believe in. What does your society give its young to believe in? There is a void at the heart of America, and it is Drac that will fill it."

"No," Lori said unshakably. She tossed her blond hair. "You're wrong."

"I'm right," asserted the prince of Wallachia. "This is a new kind of war, and the first casualties will be the children."

"But you'll be stopped," Ben said. "People'll fight you, stand against you. *We* will."

"You will." Tepesch appeared amused. "Or will you? It seems the time has come for me to put my proposition to you."

"Proposition?" Ben wondered what could possibly be next.

"Some are certainly resisting the Wallachian advance, vested interests like the ridiculous Serpents and our mutual friend Talon. Granted, I could sweep them from my sight soon enough, but I have come to America to personally supervise our final distribution network, not to be diverted by petty annoyances. Others can eliminate Talon for me — my men, with perhaps a little assistance from those with more of a direct reason to hate the scaled one. *You*, my friends."

"Us?" Ben was shocked. "Why would we help you?"

"Because I know he murdered one of your own. My men have been watching you since the brawl at the docks. I know you seek revenge, and I can help you get it. We are very close to discovering the location of the Serpents' main headquarters, their nest. When we have found it, we will strike and remove the Serpents from our path once and for all. You could be there in the vanguard of our attack, to gain justice for your fallen friend. I can give you Talon."

"Before, you talked about mutual interest," Lori recalled. "So you can do something for us. What do you expect us to do for you?"

Tepesch acknowledged Lori's question. "Technology," he

said, like it was the name of a lover. "Your technology. Clearly, you are not normal teenagers. Your fighting skills, your prowess, they tell me that. You are members of an organization of which your countrymen are not aware, no? An organization that can supply you with electrical suits and invisibility emitters and, I imagine, many similar marvels. Such technology and weaponry could prove most useful to my nation."

It was obvious to Ben what was coming now.

"You look upon Drac with revulsion, do you not? I understand that. As I have told you, my ancestors were warriors. Their blood courses in my veins. I would rather confront my enemies face to face than be forced to engage in poisonous campaigns like this. But the economic position of my country gives me no choice. Wallachia cannot fight openly against the West unless we, too, have access to your level of weapons technology." Tepesch smiled. A deceiver's smile. "Access that you can give me."

"No," said Ben.

"So that is our bargain. Talon for technology. Revenge for information."

"No," said Ben. "Didn't you hear me the first time?" He felt his teammates were with him.

"You need awhile to consider, of course." Tepesch was the generous host. "Boris will return you to your room, and we will speak again in the morning."

"Uh, Mr. Tepesch? Prince?" Eddie waved. "What if we decide, you know, what if we decide to decline your kind proposition?"

The smile did not falter, even as Tepesch's fist closed around and crushed the dracul flower, as its petals fluttered to the floor like shreds of pale skin. "Then," he said, "you would be most unwise. Most unwise, indeed."

CHAPTER FOURTEEN

"So what do we do now?" Lori said.

They'd been escorted back to their room. The door had been locked fast. Happy peasants frolicked through the Viewscenes, but then they weren't prisoners in a luxury cell from which there seemed to be no escape.

Eddie eyed up the satin-sheeted beds hopefully. "Well, if the worst comes to the worst, I think we'd better take old Vlad's advice and make the most of the time we've got." He winked at Cally.

Cally snorted. "Trouble is, Eddie, every woman I can think of'd be more than happy to die without having lain in your arms. Know what I mean?"

"No jokes," growled Jake darkly. "Let's leave dying out of it."

Cally and Eddie both thought of Jennifer. They fell silent.

"He's testing us, that's what he's doing." Ben narrowed his eyes, made them slits of piercing blue. "He's trying to confuse us. He must know we can't accept what he's offering. You deal with the devil, and you lose your soul."

"That's it," Lori added. "Vlad thinks we don't believe in anything, that our values aren't strong enough to resist him."

"Then he's made a mistake," declared Ben. "I do believe. I believe in everything this country stands for, freedom, democracy, personal responsibility —"

"That's easy for you to say, Ben," objected Cally. "You're rich. Your family's rich. Big ideas like freedom and democracy don't always seem so important when your stomach's empty and you don't know how you're going to fill it."

"Yeah? Getting a job might help," Ben retorted. "Standing on your own two feet."

"Hey, hey." Eddie stepped between them. "How about we leave the political discussion for the next presidential election campaign and work out how we're gonna live long enough to see it?"

"Ben's right about one thing, at least," contributed Jake. "We can't trust Tepesch. Choosing between the Wallachians and the Serpents is like choosing between the black death and bubonic plague."

"Aren't they the same thing?" Lori struggled to remember her history.

"Exactly. It's a fake choice," Jake said. "It's no choice. The only choice we've got is to do our own thing and trust one another. I say no deal."

"So what are we gonna say when beardy Boris turns up in a few hours, plus guns, and asks if we're onboard or not?" Eddie worried.

"We won't be saying anything," Jake pointed out. "We won't be here."

"What, someone's wearing a spare nitronail they haven't told us, about?" Eddie glanced hopefully at his teammates. "Whoever's got it, slip it on the door and let's go."

"None of us are wearing nitronails, Eddie," said Ben.

"And forget the door." Jake was already taking his own advice and pressing his palms against the wall, then rapping various sections with his knuckles. "There'll be guards outside, anyway."

"So what are you doing? Checking for a secret passage?" Eddie seemed to think the prospect of finding one unlikely.

"Not quite," said Jake. "But we know this isn't a real castle, right?" He felt and rapped, felt and rapped. "It's a Wallachian theme park in the Cultural Exchange Building. These walls aren't stone. They're fake. It's all fake." He paused, seemed to have found something. "Just like Vlad's code of so-called honor. The leader of his people. Noble protector of the nation. Noble crap. He's just a killer with a crown, and he's got a big surprise coming to him." Jake drew back his fist.

"Jake," gasped Lori, "what do you think you're . . . ?"

He smashed it into the wall.

"Ouch," winced Eddie. "That's got to hurt."

If it did, Jake betrayed no pain. In fact, he punched the wall again. The third time, it crumbled and flaked like old paintwork. "Are you gonna help then or what?"

"It's a vent!" Lori exclaimed, as if Jake had uncovered a marvelous treasure. "You've found an air vent."

"He's found a way out," Ben admired grudgingly, tearing and pulling at the damaged fabric of the wall.

"Thank the Lord for ventilation systems," sighed Eddie. "Where would a hardworking secret agent be without them?"

The ventilation duct was fully exposed now, the artificial stones in shreds around it. Jake and Ben removed the wire-mesh cover and slung it onto a bed. The vent was shoulder height and just big enough to accommodate one person at a time.

"It's going to be a squeeze, though," said Ben.

"That's okay," said Eddie. "I'm used to flying coach."

"So who's first?" As if Cally didn't know.

"I'm first." Ben was already stripping off his tuxedo and

rolling up his sleeves. Jake was doing the same. "I'm team leader. Then Lori, Eddie, Cal, and Jake. Problems?"

"You want to lose the jacket, Ed?" Jake asked.

"No way. This is the best bit of gear I've got. And what happens if we get into a situation that calls for polite conversation? The jacket stays."

"What about our dresses?" Lori looked down at the blue creation that flowed to her ankles. "They're going to reduce our mobility."

"Too true," Eddie grinned. "They'll have to come off."

"In your dreams, Nelligan," scoffed Cally.

"Listen, we don't have time for this." Ben was itching for departure. "Can't you tear them off above the knee or something? Then you'll have movement and modesty."

Cally and Lori nodded, complied. Two hoops of ripped material fluttered to the floor.

"*Now* we can leave?" Ben said.

One by one, Bond Team heaved themselves into the ventilation duct. The tunnel was dark and it was narrow, but its metal construction also made it smooth and of regular dimensions, not pleasant but certainly straightforward to crawl through. Ben set a fierce pace, forcing his limbs forward and commanding himself to ignore what would be the growing ache in his back. On missions, aches and pains were often good. They meant you were still alive.

"Everybody all right back there?" he hissed. "Lori?"

"Apart from wishing I was several inches shorter, yeah."

"Yo, Ben." It was Jake, a shape in the distant darkness. "Why are we resting?"

"I'm not resting," Ben snapped resentfully. "I'm thinking."

They'd come to a major intersection in the ventilation system. They could turn left or right, carry on in the same direction or — and this was what Ben was considering — go downward. A yawning shaft like a metallic pit led to the building's lower floors. It seemed to Ben their only option.

"You're kidding, right?" Eddie gaped, his mouth as wide as the shaft.

"Down is good," said Ben. "Down takes us closer to the ground floor. Ground floor gets us out."

"Yeah, I can follow that," said Eddie, "but if we slip and lose our footing, we'll get to the ground floor so quickly they'll be scraping us up for weeks."

"There's only one thing to do then, Ed," called Cally from behind. "Don't slip."

Ben went first, lowering himself into the shaft with the help of the tunnels left and right, ramming his feet against one side of the drop and his back against the opposite, steadying himself, balancing and groping for what grip there was with his hands and arms, shimmying slowly, carefully, precariously downward.

"Where's a spray of clingskin when you need it?" somebody complained.

Lori followed, having first removed her shoes and hung them over her wrists by the straps: High heels were not intended for excursions in ventilation shafts. Eddie grumbled himself into position next, the only consolation he could think of was that if he slipped and fell, he'd land on top of Lori. Cally inched her way down with minimum fuss and Jake, last in line, paused only to peer back the way they'd come. No sign of pursuit so far, which was encouraging. If only it would last . . .

Ben wouldn't have admitted it to the others, scarcely liked

to admit it to himself, but he was considerably relieved when there was finally solid metal beneath him again. He thought he was in good physical condition, but right now his limbs were wobbling as if the bones had been removed. He sprawled out in the tunnel and gasped.

"You all right, Ben?" Lori dropped alongside him. She didn't even seem to be breathing hard, and yet not long ago, she'd been in a hospital bed with fang marks in her throat. How did she do it?

"Look. Up there," she shouted. "More grilles. We might be able to break out, or at least get our bearings."

"Did somebody mention 'breaks'?" Eddie moaned, as he joined them. "My back's breaking, does that count?"

"Shut up, Eddie!" Ben hissed. "We don't want anyone to hear us." He nodded ahead to Lori. "Let's take a look."

They crawled to the farthest of the two wire-mesh grilles and peered into a long, narrow room banked high with computers and monitors, screens, and keyboards. "Control center?" Ben didn't have to be Sherlock Holmes to make the guess. Lori was more concerned with the presence of Vlad Tepesch among the room's occupants, his black cloak like a clue to his soul and setting him apart from the technicians who carried out their functions in the palest of garments. Boris, dutifully, stood at his master's right hand.

"Well?" For once, Tepesch seemed impatient. "You said there was news, important news."

Ben indicated in mime that Eddie, Cally, and Jake should look out through the second of the vents but that they should do so silently. Anything important for Vlad was probably vital for them.

"We have located the Serpents' nest," declared a technician. "Our surveillance team in Undertown detected the return of Talon to his headquarters."

"Excellent," Tepesch gloated. "Show me."

It was the moon. The screens displayed the artificial moon above Undertown as it glowed uncertainly in the night. Then, rising toward it, was a hover-deck, one of the floating platforms that workers used to access the moon in order to carry out repairs and other maintenance. Only this hover-deck did not carry workers. Even from the ventilation duct, Bond Team could see that. One of the disadvantages of Talon's scales was that he couldn't really lose himself in a crowd. The moon opened up to receive him, great, gleaming metal panels parting so that the hover-deck could enter the orb. Vlad Tepesch needed to witness no longer.

"How long ago was this?" he demanded. "Where is Talon now?"

"According to our surveillance team," the technician said, "he remains inside the satellite. This film was taken less than an hour ago, my prince."

"Excellent," Vlad Tepesch repeated. "Then we can bring this charade to an end before daybreak and finally eliminate the Serpent threat. Prepare an assault on the Undertown moon immediately. Dispatch all available forces. We will snare the Serpent in his nest."

"At once, my prince."

"Oh, and before you do, let those wretched children know that their time for consideration has just been cut short."

"Does he mean us?" whispered Eddie offendedly. "Wretched? A bit harsh, isn't it?"

"And on their decision depend their lives."

"Yes, my prince," bowed Boris, and hastened from the room.

"I think that's our cue as well," breathed Ben. "When they find we've gone . . ."

With renewed vigor, Bond Team continued their crawl through the ventilation system. "Let's keep it moving up the front there," Jake urged. "If they start following us, guess who's first in line for trouble."

"If you want to swap places, Daly, just say the word," Ben called back in annoyance. "It's not that there's any sign up here reading 'This Way Out.'"

"I don't know," said Lori. "Maybe there is, Ben. Look."

Lori's sharp eyes had seen it first. The end of the tunnel and another shaft dropping down, but this one had metal rungs set into one wall. Ben found he didn't care that somebody else had spotted it before him — much. "A central maintenance shaft," he grinned. "I'm betting it goes all the way to the ground floor. Who's for finding out?"

Unanimous.

They emerged from the shaft into a maintenance room stacked with odd pieces of equipment just as the wail of an alarm rang through the building, like the cry of someone who's just realized he's been robbed.

"Do you think that's for us?" Cally wondered.

"Maybe they just test the alarm every now and then," Eddie suggested.

"Maybe we don't want to find out." Jake joined Ben and Lori who were easing open the maintenance room's door. "What are we looking at, Lo?"

"The jackpot." Lori grinned. "Ladies and gentlemen, your transport awaits."

The room opened out onto the garages. Hoverlimos were lined up like soldiers for inspection, including several that bore pennants of the Wallachian flag on their pristine, polished hoods. But Bond Team's taste did not run to limousines. More to their liking was the trio of SkyBikes parked nearby.

"There is a God," declared Eddie, "and he loves me!"

"We must be in the sub-levels," Ben said. "Basement parking."

Eddie was already at the bikes, stroking them like pets. Skybiking was one area where he was the acknowledged expert, where he didn't have to hide behind one-liners and buffoonery. On these machines, Eddie Nelligan was king.

"Then get them started," Ben ordered, "before we get company." The alarm was still reverberating through the garage. "Three bikes, three teams. Me and Lori, Cally and Jake, Eddie on his own."

"How is Eddie on his own a team?" the boy in question queried as his deft and skillful fingers hot-wired the first bike. The magnetically powered engine purred seductively into life.

"Someone's got to fly alone," Ben pointed out, "and you're about the best —"

"No." Jake said it like a hammer blow.

"No?" As if Ben hadn't heard right. "I don't —"

"Eddie's not going on his own." Jake was thinking of Talon in the moon, and the Wallachians closing in to deny him his just vengeance for Jennifer's death. Escape for Tepesch was only the first thing on Jake's mind. "I am."

"You're not." Ben didn't like to be contradicted at the best of times, but with alarm bells ringing and Wallachian guards bound to appear at any moment . . . "I've told you the teams, Jake, and that's it."

"Jake, what's the matter?" Lori frowned.

"That's not it, Stanton." He glanced across to where Eddie had now coaxed the second bike to life. "That's not even close."

Later, Lori realized that it had been obvious what was coming next, but at the time, Jake suddenly leaping into the saddle of the first SkyBike was something of a shock. "Daly, what . . . ?" from Ben and, "Mind my head, it's the only one I've got!" from Eddie as Jake reared the machine into the air like he was participating in a techno-rodeo.

"I'm going after Talon," he yelled to his astonished teammates. "You can follow if you want, but if anyone's gonna get him, it's gonna be me."

"Jake, you can't!" Ben grabbed at thin air as Jake revved up the SkyBike and shot away.

"I guess he thinks he can," said Cally and, eyes widening, "I guess we should think about joining him."

Wallachian guards were spilling into the room, maybe half a dozen of them.

Ben, Lori, and Cally ducked down by the SkyBikes. The guards would take only seconds to find their range and cover the distance between them and Bond Team.

And then Eddie was exulting as the SkyBike's engine fired.

For once, Cally could have kissed him.

"They can still pick us off before we get airborne!" Lori cried.

"Uh-uh," grinned Eddie. "These are weapons-grade bikes." The guards were getting closer, charging straight at them. "And Vlad's goons should be coming into range just about . . ." Eddie's fingers snaked to a button on the nearest bike's central control panel. "Now!"

He pressed the button. Laser blasts spat from the bike's

undercarriage. The limousines with the pennants exploded, the force of the eruption scattering the guards.

"Now can we go?" Cally said.

"Absolutely." Ben was already astride one bike, Lori mounting behind him. "Ride like the wind."

"Do you fancy driving?" Eddie asked Cally politely, Ben and Lori rising above them and keeping the sprawled Wallachians pinned down with further laser blasts. "That way I get to hold on to you, Cal."

"Yeah?" Cally didn't need a second invitation. She gripped the handlebars with pleasure. "Then hold on tight, Eddie. This is gonna be wild."

Cally accelerated with a whoosh of power that almost left Eddie dangling.

"Not too high in here!" he wailed from behind. "Ceilings tend to be solid, Cal."

"Then keep your head down!" She sped in a perfectly straight line, sparse inches below the garage roof. "Back-seat drivers!"

They were rapidly approaching the exit. It had been barred and guarded, but Jake, Ben, and Lori had taken care of that. Flames burned among the debris. But now a thick metal shield was lowering itself from the ceiling, impregnable to laser fire. It would cut off their escape, seal them in. Cally had only one chance. "You know how I said hold on tight, Eddie?"

"I have it in writing."

"Yeah? Well, I mean it!"

Cally suddenly tilted the bike to forty-five degrees, swooped low. She heard Eddie shouting out. She was shouting out. The shield above, the ground below. Cold air slapping at her face and her stomach heaved, but one single daring, dramatic moment and they were through. And now the shield was preventing any immediate pursuit.

The Wallachian building was behind them. City lights were scattered before them like stars as they climbed to join Ben and Lori hovering in wait several stories above the street. There was no sign of Jake.

"What kept you?" Lori yelled.

"A close encounter with a metal door," Cally returned, "but we got through it okay."

"Speak for yourself," Eddie groaned queasily. "I think I'm about to have a close encounter with my breakfast."

"Shut up, Eddie," scolded Ben. "We've got to decide what to do next."

"I suppose calling for reinforcements is out of the question," Eddie said. "I mean, these things have got communicators."

"No, that's exactly what we need to do. Contact Grant." Ben shook his head. "I don't like to say it, but this thing is getting too big for us."

"What about Jake, though?" Lori pressed. "We can't let him take on Talon alone." Hanging in the air unspoken: *You know what happened to the last one of us that tried it.*

"He shouldn't have just flown off like that." Ben was adopting the do-it-by-the-book line. "We're supposed to be a team."

"He's thinking of Jennifer," Cally said. "You can't blame him, Ben."

"Navigator function'll take us straight to the Undertown moon," Eddie informed them. "If that's the way we want to go."

"Ben?" Lori's lips were pleading at his ear.

"All right. All right," Ben consented, though not entirely happy. "We go after Jake. I'll let Spy High know what's happening en route."

The two SkyBikes revved up to full speed and streaked across the Los Angeles night.

CHAPTER FIFTEEN

What must she have been thinking, Jake wondered, *when she realized that there was no way out? What was on Jennifer's mind when she knew she was going to die?*

With hectic, dizzying speed, he raced above the gulfs and canyons of the skyscraper city.

Did her life flash before her eyes, as tradition claimed happened to those on the brink of death? If not, what did Jennifer see? Darkness? Total and unutterable? The void into which she was falling?

He kept his head low, his legs clamped tightly to the sides of the machine. The night was a deep pit beneath him, a chasm. It was a long way down.

But if so, what did she remember? What moments from her fourteen years, what replays of the past returned to give her strength as she faced her final moment? Was I one of them?

He burst through the advids like an arrow through a balloon, was splashed briefly with their unnatural colors like blood in green and white and blue. And red. Red was the color of the world. A perfect blond woman opened her mouth to express delight at something she'd just swallowed; Jake burst from between her teeth, scarring her smile.

The bike was at its limits, juddering with effort, but he had to get there quickly, before the Wallachians robbed him of his revenge, of Jennifer's revenge. He'd let her down in life, hadn't been there when she'd needed him, but he wouldn't this time. He'd finish what she'd started, he swore it.

The bike's navigator system indicated that his journey was all but over.

Jake's eyes corroborated the fact.

The Undertown moon hovered before him, and from his vantage point, he could see that it was not a perfect circle at all, but a multifaceted globe composed of hundreds of flat hexagonal plates, each one several meters across and welded at the edges to its neighbors. Each seemed capable of generating its own glowing light source, and many, if not every one, could apparently be opened to provide an aperture wide enough for men to stand in, to stand in and to fire weapons from. Which seemed a highly desirable quality just at the moment.

The moon was under attack.

Spy High students were trained to assimilate as much information as possible from a single glance at any scene. There was plenty for Jake to observe from the pandemonium unfolding before him now. Assault helicopters, at least half a dozen of them, whirred and buzzed around the moon like a swarm of angry black and red wasps. They spat rockets that flared against the paneled surface of the globe, damaging, denting, but not yet perforating the massive structure. Pulsar fire from weapons mounted at the front of the choppers scored violent patterns on the face of the moon, like deadly tattoos, and picked off the Serpent defenders where it could. Some zealous Wallachians shot at their foes from the open flanks of the helicopters, making targets of themselves. Serpents blazed back at their attackers with laser weapons of their own.

Jake flitted between the combatants, desperate not to place himself within the line of fire. The Wallachians hated the Serpents. The Serpents hated the Wallachians. That was the nature of a war. But both sides hated him. Jake wondered fleetingly whether he ought not to have waited for the others, but they might have tried to talk him out of it, and he couldn't have that. Talon was inside that globe, cowering or defiant it didn't matter. Jake was not only prepared but also glad to risk his life in order to reach him.

And he would reach him. Somehow.

Gunfire scorched past his ears. A missile from the moon. It hit the rotor blades of a helicopter almost directly above him and ignited. Jake whisked to one side as the doomed chopper lurched past, the pilot struggling to regain control.

One Wallachian down, but they'd win sooner or later, Jake realized. They had greater maneuverability and greater firepower. So if he wanted to get to Talon first . . .

He assessed his options.

One: landing on the roof of the moon.

But two Wallachian choppers already had the same idea; they were hovering above and dangling ladders for soldiers to descend. Serpents climbed through open panels from within the moon to stop them. That route was too busy for Jake.

Then a Wallachian shell finally ruptured the globe's skin, tore a hole in its side, and he had his second option — smash his way in. Jake liked the sound of that. It matched his mood.

He gunned his bike away from the battle, building up speed. Took a deep breath and veered around in an arc like a scythe, swinging back toward the burning moon. The bike shuddered, maybe in fear.

Jake gritted his teeth, picked his spot, opened up with his lasers.

There was wind in his face, chaos wild around him.

The moon loomed up, punching at him like a sudden fist.

Acceleration.

Hold on.

His laser blasts pummeled into the panel but it wasn't yielding. They'd be scraping him up tomorrow like jam.

Pull out. No way. *You'll die.* No way.

Impact soon.

The cracks appeared, fissures, lines, like the shattering shell of an egg.

He was going to do it. He was going to break through.

Impact now. He couldn't look.

Jennifer . . .

"Did you see that? Ben, did you see that?" Lori's hair streamed behind her as she cried out in horror. "Jake's rammed the moon. He's burst his way inside . . . He's crazy!" But she seemed thrilled nonetheless.

"We trying the same, Ben?" Cally wanted to know.

The two bikes had made swift progress. Both Ben and Cally were superior SkyBikers to Jake and had Spy High credits to prove it, but whether either possessed the nerve to follow his lead was more debatable.

"Not wise," Ben decided. "He might be injured or something, and we'd be the same. Jake can go that route. We'll play the percentages."

"How d'you mean?" Cally said.

Ben jabbed a finger upward, to a helicopter above them. "Up for some sky-jacking?"

* * *

He was hurting, but there seemed to be nothing broken. He was bleeding, but they were only scratches. Flesh wounds didn't count.

Jake was on his back on a hard metal surface. His vision was dazed, hazy, not helped by the smoke that billowed from the moon's interior. But he could just make out, from the corner of his eye, the mangled ruins of his SkyBike.

The Serpent standing over him with a pulse rifle was pretty clear, too.

Jake didn't mess around. He kicked out, sweeping the man from his feet, catching his falling pulse rifle and flicking the setting to stun in one slick motion.

One less Serpent to worry about.

Not that the thug's comrades seemed unduly concerned about Jake's presence, in any case. The assault of the Wallachian helicopters seemed a more pressing priority. The scene inside the moon reminded Jake of pictures he'd seen at school of the gun deck of an embattled sailing ship in olden days, all scurrying and smoke and panic and pain. Modern weapons had replaced cannon and machetes, and the vessel was made of metal rather than oak, but the effect was the same. And he could tell that the Serpent cause was sinking fast.

And then Jake saw him — through the railings and the stairwell that led between levels, on the next landing up, tall and commanding still, barking orders, shaven-headed and naked to the waist as ever. Talon.

It was show time.

They'd done it in the Spyscapes, boarded one flying vehicle from another, but in virtual reality, however hard as you might try to ignore it, the undeniable truth was that if you slipped and fell screaming to your death from a great height, the only damage done would be to your ego, and even public humiliation was something you could recover from. To attempt to board a helicopter from a SkyBike in the middle of an all-out assault on an artificial moon, in real time, in real life, was rather different. The consequences of failure were likely to be more severe.

After all, reality didn't come with second chances. Ask Jennifer.

But they wouldn't need second chances, Ben determined. They had their training, and he was a Stanton besides. Failure wasn't in his personal dictionary. Timing, however, was.

He glanced across to Cally and Eddie's SkyBike, flying directly parallel with his and Lori's but at a little distance, a helicopter's width. Above them a chopper whirred, firing its rockets at the moon. At Ben's signal, they rose toward it in perfect unison.

Ben directed his gaze upward now. The helicopter's side doors were open. A pair of Wallachians were firing pulse rifles from there, more to look good than for any material harm they might cause to the Serpents. If all went well, they weren't going to be looking too good in a moment.

In the wind currents, in the maelstrom caused by the chopper's rotor blades, Ben fought to keep his SkyBike level. "All right, Lo," he indicated. "Get ready."

She did. Keeping a tight grip on Ben's shoulders, she drew up first one leg and then the other until she was squatting, precariously balanced, on the bike's saddle behind him. "I should have been in the circus!" she joked. She didn't look down. That was the trick, Lori had learned. That was how you survived anything at altitude. You never looked down.

"Okay," Ben called. "Going up!"

It was the final, vital movement. A sudden rise. SkyBikes appearing on both sides of the chopper simultaneously, startling its Wallachian occupants. Then Lori and Eddie were springing, madly, suicidally, from their saddles across the yawning gulf of space, as if defying gravity itself.

They landed safely inside the body of the helicopter, not even pausing for breath. The Wallachians hardly had time to register their astonishment.

"What's going on back there?" The copilot tried to swivel in his seat to get a clearer look.

"Nothing you need to worry about." Lori's well-aimed karate chop put the man temporarily beyond emotions of any kind.

The pilot grabbed for a shock blaster. "Keep both hands on the controls, please," Eddie said, disabling his right arm, "or we won't let you fly anymore. In fact, we think it's time you let someone else have a turn, anyway. Namely, us." He prodded in a pressure point in the pilot's neck, and the pilot slumped gently forward against the window. "Care to take the wheel, Lori?"

"Love to, Eddie." She clambered over the pilot and addressed herself to the controls. The helicopter was a model she'd handled in simulations a hundred times. Eddie hauled the unconscious pilot out of the way and Lori settled into her seat comfortably. "Thanks."

"My pleasure. Just hold her steady while I help our final passengers aboard."

"As a rock," promised Lori.

Which was just as well. For Ben and Cally to leap from the SkyBikes was even more dangerous than it had been for their passengers. Cally came first, sliding her left leg over so that she was riding almost sidesaddle, then launching herself for the chopper and Eddie's welcoming arms. The bike spiraled toward collision with the ground. Cally's momentum nearly knocked Eddie over. "Hmm," he said. "The night's looking up."

"If your hands aren't somewhere else in a microsecond, Eddie," warned Cally breathlessly and not without humor, "you'll be joining our Wallachian friends on the floor."

"Ah, Cal, don't be like that —"

"Hey!" Ben yelled angrily from alongside the helicopter. "If you two have got a spare moment, I'd sooner not spend the rest of this mission holding on to a SkyBike single-handedly!"

"All right then, Ben." Cally was quickly into position to receive him. "Jump!"

Ben did, but maybe he slightly misjudged the distance, or maybe the fact that he was heavier than Cally sent his SkyBike into its final nosedive more quickly, or maybe something else entirely, but Ben didn't make the helicopter, not all the way.

He felt himself falling, floundering in midair, flapping useless arms like a bird that couldn't fly. He saw Eddie's features transformed from amusement into anxiety, Cally's lunge to catch him.

He stabbed out his arms. They slammed onto the solid metal floor of the chopper. But his legs were dangling, struggling to find support but failing. His grip slipped, too, his fingernails scraping metal, his weight dragging him toward death. "Hel . . ." He nearly said it. Benjamin T. Stanton Jr. nearly said it.

Then Cally's hands clamped around one arm, Eddie's around the other. They pulled him aboard like an anchor. He wasn't going to fall. He wasn't going to die.

He was going to have to be grateful.

"Now, sir, I hope you've got a valid ticket," said Eddie.

"Talon!"

He could have taken him out then and there. In all the chaos and confusion, Jake could simply have taken steady aim with his appropriate pulse rifle and blasted the leader of the Serpents right off the moon. Surely, even Talon's Kevlar skin couldn't repel a pulse blast. But was that the kind of justice he wanted for Jennifer? Did he really want her memory to be associated with shooting a man in the back? Jake didn't think so. He wanted the scaled man to know who had bested him and why.

So he spat out the name like a foul taste, like a curse: "Talon!"

And Talon turned, sensing the fury in the voice, recognizing its owner. He turned to face Jake as his empire crumbled around him.

"You? *Again?*" Bafflement or a grudging admiration, Jake didn't know or care. "Don't you ever give up?"

"You're the one who'd better give up," warned Jake, his fingers itching to press the trigger in spite of himself. "And now would be a good time. Before I lose control of my right hand."

"What, and kill me? You wouldn't just shoot me like that, would you?" Talon was sly, cunning. He hadn't attained his lofty position by panicking at each new threat, and this was only a child. "In cold blood? According to your rules, that would make you just as bad as me, wouldn't it?"

"Nobody can be as bad as you," scorned Jake, "and who says I'm playing by the rules?"

"Go ahead, then," Talon invited. "Give it your best shot. Your girlfriend tried to take me with her bare hands. She failed, of course. So will you."

Jake's eyes narrowed in icy resolve. "Don't bet on it. I'm warning you Talon. This is your last —"

The moon suddenly lurched, suddenly rocked. Jake swayed, lost balance. "Stabilizers!" someone shouted.

Talon was on him, pulverizing quickly, knocking him to the floor with a booted foot in the ribs. Jake's rifle was kicked away. "Better luck next time, boy," the scaled man scorned.

Then he was gone, fled, but not from Jake. From the increasing carnage surrounding them both. Jake forced himself to his knees, saw Talon snapping orders to a subordinate, indicating up, saw him dart to the steps that led higher, to the very roof of the globe. Was he going to try to escape that way, get picked up or something? Jake couldn't allow it. He stood. He forced the pain in his ribs to subside. The moon was balanced again but for how long?

It didn't matter. Jake loped into a run. He didn't need long to track Talon down.

"Hold on!" warned Lori, banking the chopper steadily as a Serpent missile seared close.

"You want me to take them out, leader man?" Eddie seemed keen to fire the rockets.

"We can't attack the moon," Ben said. "Jake's in there somewhere, and we can't risk endangering him by accident."

"So what do we do?" Eddie demanded. "Admire the view?"

"Look!" Cally saw them first. Talon was on the roof of the moon. He'd climbed out of one of the open parcels and was searching the skies for something. Not far behind him, Jake. Both of them dived to the ground as two Wallachian helicopters raked the surface with laser fire. The battle here was already well and truly joined.

"They're our targets!" Ben cried. "The Wallachian choppers. Before they get to Jake!"

"Your wish is my command, O Great One." Eddie grinned.

He fired, crippling the first Wallachian helicopter. Its crew bailed out as the machine dropped like a stone, crashing into the side of the moon as it did. The second, now alerted to this surprise source of attack, retracted the ladder it had been in the process of lowering and blazed its guns at the Bond Teamers.

"Hold on!" warned Lori again.

"That's what I like about Lo," observed Eddie. "She makes such great conversation."

Jake had little idea what was going on in the skies above him or that his teammates were so close. He didn't even notice the lasers that hissed around him. He had eyes only for Talon, and they were cold eyes, too, like death.

He was without a weapon now, but it didn't seem to matter. Maybe his need for revenge would be weapon enough.

"Still?" Talon immediately assumed a defensive posture, but there was a weary disbelief about him now. "How long does it take for you to realize that I cannot be beaten by the likes of you?"

"You're not looking too hot from where I'm standing, big man."

Talon glanced to the sky, the darkness paling as dawn approached. "I've no time to kill you now, Jake."

"What? When the going gets tough, the tough get going? Running away's going to ruin your reputation, Talon."

"Back off now, boy, and I'll let you live."

Jake glared, tensed for combat. "No deal."

"Then I'll just have to kill you before my transport arrives."

He struck like lightning, cobra-quick, but Jake was expecting the assault, reduced a paralyzing punch to a glancing blow, chopped at Talon's neck himself. The skin was like steel. Talon lashed back and caught Jake under the chin. His sight seemed to explode, and he realized he'd been knocked to the ground, to the arching, trembling surface of the moon. He gasped, shook his head to clear it. Talon was right. Immune from harm in his armored flesh, there was no way that normal fists, however strong, could stop him.

Jake needed a plan B, like now.

Talon almost on top of him, lit red from behind in a fireball flare. Jake's head was dizzied by the blow he'd received and his altitude high above the hard, unyielding city streets. The kick he rolled to avoid. Easy to roll on a globe, to find a slope, to use it. The curve of the moon dropping away into darkness, a rounded, paneled precipice.

Jake urged himself onto unwavering feet. He'd got plan B.

But Talon didn't seem to want to know. He wasn't pressing his attack but withdrawing, signaling, waving his arms above his head like a castaway to a ship.

A helicopter threaded through battle toward him.

Jake shook his head. He wasn't going to be cheated again. He threw himself at Talon's waist, like tackling a truck. Talon was propelled forward but not far enough, and now Jake was too close to those smashing, hammer-like fists. They cudgeled his shoulder, his head. He felt the gorge rise but he had to hold on. Had to. For Jennifer.

"Will —" pounding — "you —" punishing — "let —" pulverizing — "go!"

Talon wrenched himself free.

"No!" Jake groped and groveled on the ground, through a scarlet haze saw Talon striding away from him. "No!" Saw the helicopter swooping low, Talon's ticket out of here.

Couldn't move. Had to move.

The ladder was dangling within Talon's grasp, his escape mere seconds away. The Serpent was tall, grinning, triumphant even in defeat.

Or not.

The rescue helicopter veered away sharply, a gaping hole in its flank.

It would have been difficult to tell who was most stupefied, Talon or Jake. But it was easy to decide who was most gratified. Only Jake burst into laughter.

They rose above the moon like silver birds of prey. Electronic voices crackled for both warring parties to lay down their weapons. The authorities had arrived.

Eddie cheered. "You've done it, Lori! You've scared him off!"

"Yeah?" Lori was doubtful. Her every maneuver had been matched and countered by the Wallachian chopper so far. It was beginning to look as if he had her measure. But it did also seem that he'd suddenly lost the stomach for a fight and had opted for total retreat. "It doesn't make sense."

"Maybe he wants to goad us into a trap?" Cally suggested.

"Maybe he got a look at Eddie's face," said Ben, "though it's likelier he saw the writing on the wall. Ben had noticed them first, but now the others could also make them out — at least half a dozen police hovertanks advancing toward them.

Eddie cheered again. "That's one beautiful sight, isn't it? I think I could almost reach out and kiss 'em." He puckered up in preparation.

The police opened fire.

"Doesn't look like the feeling's mutual!" Cally observed.

"Hold on!" Lori took evasive action.

"If she says that one more time . . ." Eddie muttered.

"Ben, why are they attacking?"

"'Cause they're not psychic, Lori. They don't see us, just a Wallachian chopper with a death wish. Cally, get on the radio. Let 'em know we're the good guys."

"Yeah, and Cal?" added Eddie. "Let 'em know it soon."

From somewhere, Jake found the strength to stand. The laughter had felt good. It had felt like adrenaline. The final Wallachian helicopters were retreating. The final Serpents were emerging from the moon's innards and raising their hands in surrender. It was over.

Correction. Almost over.

"Looks like you're staying after all," Jake confronted Talon. "And hear that?" As the police voices repeated their demands. "That's the sound of lights out for you."

"Really?" Talon's expression contorted with hatred. "Then I've nothing to lose, have I? It's time for you and your pretty little girlfriend to be reunited."

Jennifer. Jake knew Talon would taunt him with the memory of Jennifer, use her to cloud his judgment, make him reckless, likelier to make mistakes. He also knew it wouldn't work. It wasn't that he no longer felt the rage and the grief that had been in him since Jen's death — he did — but they were somehow harnessed now, a source of strength rather than weakness. They would help him and keep him safe. Jake prepared himself. He was strong. He didn't need scales or tattoos or body armor or anything artificial to defeat Talon. He knew that now. His own spirit would suffice.

And as Talon lunged at him, he realized that it was the Serpent who was now at the mercy of his emotions. The nearly hooded eyes blazed like madness. The mouth was fixed in a feral snarl. His limbs quivered with barely controlled fury.

Jake sidestepped neatly. Talon floundered, flailed. Jake didn't even attempt a blow of his own. Talon was too powerful, but that power could be used against him. What Talon couldn't hit, he couldn't hurt.

"Missed," said Jake, "but if you want to try again, I'm over here now. Hi."

Talon took another swipe at empty air and then another. "You're only delaying the inevitable, boy," he fumed. But his attacks were losing discipline now, becoming the desperate forays of a punch-drunk boxer in his final fight.

Jake felt a distance from his body. He felt serene, uplifted, effortlessly confident. He felt that Jennifer was with him, guiding him, lending her soul to his.

He led Talon further across the moon, the surface dipping away sharply behind him.

"Your pretty little girlfriend didn't run, Jake," Talon jeered.

What he said didn't matter. It was the wind that whipped around Jake's body that mattered, and the steep, falling angle behind him, and the slickness of the moon's surface that would allow no handhold, not even to fingers covered with Kevlar.

"Who's running?" Jake said. "Come and get me, big man."

Talon leapt. So did Jake. But where Talon launched himself high, Jake went low. He felt the Serpent's fingers raking at his shirt but gaining no purchase. He heard a cry of realization welling from Talon's throat as the solid surface ran out. He turned to see if the man had plummeted to his death.

But not quite. Not yet.

Talon was slipping, sliding, his weight dragging him further into the fatal grip of gravity. And was that fear at last in the Serpent's eyes? "Listen to me! Jake?" Squirming helplessly. "You can't just let me fall!" From this height, he'd need significantly more than armored skin to save him. "If you let me fall . . . it'll be murder!"

"Yeah, and you'd know all about murder, wouldn't you?"

All he had to do was wait now. He didn't have to lift a finger. All he had to do was stand there and admire the view like somebody out for a stroll while another human being dropped to his death. Simple.

Only not so simple. Jake couldn't just stand there, couldn't wait and watch another human being die, not even one as loathsome as Talon, not when by reaching out his hand, he could save him.

He hoped that Jennifer would understand.

"Hold on." Jake scrambled into a kneeling position, steadied himself as far as was possible, extended his hand tentatively toward Talon. "I'll pull you up."

"You'd help me?" Talon marveled. "After everything?"

"Don't expect me to like it," said Jake.

"Then you're a fool!"

And Talon's hand stabbed at Jake's, lashed out to seize him, to yank him down, to throw him from the moon. But Jake was faster. Their fingers brushed but then he was propelling himself backward, and Talon was clutching only air and scrabbling hopelessly for safety. His sudden movement had almost been his last.

He didn't scream. Talon didn't make another sound. He simply slithered off the side of the moon, like a snake. Jake didn't see him hit the ground. He didn't need to.

"You can rest easy now, Jen," he whispered. "It's over."

"Jake?"

Somehow, Senior Tutor Elmore Grant was behind him. Jake was taken aback. Apparently, the Undertown moon was now once again in the possession of the proper authorities.

"Talon? Ben's filled me in."

"I'm afraid he got away, sir." Jake indicated the drop. "Kind of." He watched the police helicopters in the sky, their rotors gleaming in the first faint rays of the coming dawn. "So I guess we're finished here, then, sir?"

"Not exactly," said Grant.

CHAPTER SIXTEEN

Jake hadn't needed to tell the others that Talon was no longer with them. They'd been able to guess that much by translating the grim satisfaction in his eyes. Anything else they might have wanted to know, and Eddie for one had a penchant for the gory detail, was going to have to wait. They'd been returned to their swish Uptown hotel before the cleanup operation at the moon had been completed, with Grant calling for a briefing in one of the conference rooms immediately after they'd showered and changed. It seemed there was still work to do.

"You might be wondering how I got here so swiftly," Grant began, "if I'd traveled back to Deveraux as I'd told you."

"Is there a clue in the 'if,' sir?" said Cally.

"Indeed." A small smile fluttered at Grant's lips. "You have the makings of a fine spy, Cally. The fact is I never actually left Los Angeles. Mr. Deveraux thought it best that I stay, to be on hand should any situation arise that might require my assistance."

"I guess a pitched battle around the Undertown moon pretty much qualifies as a 'situation,'" said Eddie.

"We were holding our own, though, sir," Ben was quick to add. "I mean, I called for backup as a precautionary measure, but we knew what we were doing. We were following our training."

"Of course, Ben. Nobody is questioning Bond Team's performance in this matter." Grant nodded approvingly. "In fact, you've been able to achieve something that none of our other agents have."

"What's that, sir?" said Lori.

"You've been inside the Wallachian Cultural Exchange Building. Oh, we've long suspected a link between President Tepesch and Drac, but he covers his tracks so well, and his men are so unblinkingly loyal that even those we capture would sooner die than implicate their 'prince.' It's made proof a problem." Grant sighed, ran his hands through his hair. "But even if we had proof, it would still be virtually impossible to act."

"Why?" Jake said bluntly. The idea of criminals escaping unpunished did not sit well with him. It offended his sense of justice.

It seemed to do the same for Grant. "Why? Because as the ruler of an independent state, Tepesch is protected from prosecution by diplomatic immunity. None of our agencies can touch him. By the same token, we can't enter the Cultural Exchange Building whatever might be going on inside without appropriate Wallachian authorization, which I doubt we're ever likely to receive. Legally, Tepesch can produce as much Drac as he likes in there, and we can't do a thing about it. Legally, our hands are tied."

"And that's the system?" Jake scorned.

"I'm afraid it is."

"Then the system sucks." And for once, not even Ben thought to disagree.

"You said legally, though, sir. Twice." Cally seemed to be majoring on the analysis of language. "What about illegally?"

"What about illegally is why we're having this briefing," said Grant. He regarded his five charges coolly, levelly. "You've been inside the building once. You know something of its layout, where they're manufacturing Drac. What about illegally means, how do you fancy a second visit?"

"Are you kidding, Mr. Grant? Excellent!" Eddie crowed. "I

had such a great time before. Maybe I can get myself another jacket."

"We'd do anything you want, sir," said Ben grandly. "It's our duty."

"Tepesch is just Talon with another face," growled Jake. "Murderers, lunatics — they're all the same."

"We've seen what Drac can do, sir," recalled Cally with a shudder. "Let's put an end to it."

"A little cultural exchange of our own," said Lori.

Vlad Tepesch, Prince of Wallachia, sat enthroned in the banquet hall where, two nights ago, he had entertained the five strange American teenagers. But no entertaining was due to take place tonight. The great table and its finely carved chairs had been removed. Other than his own throne, the room was now bare of furniture, devoid of life. Torches cast flickering shadows on the stone walls and vaulted ceiling, shadows like restless ghosts. Vlad Tepesch sat motionlessly, as if in a trance, his eyes deep and dark and unfathomable.

"Excuse me, my prince." The voice of a servant who scarcely dared to enter the hall. "Everything is ready for departure."

The words seemed to waken Tepesch, to activate him. His head turned slightly to observe the servant. "Good. Good."

The servant bowed thoughtfully and retreated. Silence again settled in the banquet hall.

Then Tepesch chuckled, as at some private joke, like the sound of cemetery leaves. "It's all right," he coaxed. "You can come out now." There was no response, largely because there seemed to be nobody within earshot to respond. But Tepesch persevered. "I know you're here. Drac in its purest form heightens a man's senses to an extraordinary level. I can hear you. Come. Let me see you, too."

"Whatever you say, Tepesch." Ben's voice. "No more games."

In three places before the throne, the air seemed to turn to water. Tepesch smiled at his own perception. To his left, Jake. To his right, Lori. Ahead of him, Ben. They wore more of the electrified suits he'd already seen, and those mechanisms on their forearms that rendered them invisible. "Welcome," said the prince of Wallachia.

"I guess you're the man when it comes to playing hide-and-seek," said Jake.

"Everything ready for departure, Tepesch?" Lori echoed the servant. "Leaving so soon? And we're barely acquainted."

"The stench of this land and the people in its distresses me," said Tepesch. "I wish to feel the good soil of Wallachia beneath my feet once more."

"Yeah?" Ben was combative. "And what? You think we're just gonna let you leave with a wave and a cheery word after all the poison you've pumped into our streets?"

Tepesch chuckled again. "And what? Do you think the three of you can stop me?"

"Maybe," Ben said. He drew a shock blaster from its holster, Jake and Lori following suit. "With a little help from our friends."

Shock blasters evidently didn't impress princes of Wallachia. Tepesch sat unmoved. His legs might have been paralyzed. "Your friends, yes. Where are your two companions, the black girl and the boy with the mouth?"

"Oh, you'll be hearing from them very soon," informed Ben.

Explosions, muffled by distance, rumbled through the room.

"Cally and Eddie say hi," Jake commented.

Tepesch inclined his head to show that he understood. "They're destroying the labs," he said. "Of course. But do you think this is the only place where Drac can be produced?"

"Look on it as a promising start," replied Ben. "And by the way, a little fact that might have escaped your notice, *my prince.* Local fire prevention regulations override even diplomatic immunity. In other words, members of the fire service and all related authorities have the right to enter any property where there's a fire, and Cally and Eddie are stoking up a big one. I bet the cops are at your door right now. I wonder what they'll find."

Tepesch's eyes narrowed. "You seem to have thought of everything," he said, "except how you intend to make it out of this room alive."

"With you as our hostage?" Lori suggested, pointing her blaster.

"I think not," said Tepesch. "Drac can provide other abilities, too." And suddenly he moved.

He was a blur among the room's guttering shadows, a streak of night in the blackness of his cloak. Before Ben could even discharge his weapon the man was on him and swatting him aside as if he were nothing. He was towering, tall, and unstoppable. He bore down on Ben, fingers like steel bands clamping around his throat, squeezing. And Ben's blaster was out of reach. There was nothing he could do.

Luckily, the same was not true for Lori and Jake. They fired in unison. And in unison they missed, but Tepesch saved himself only by darting away from Ben, giving him a chance to recover, and Jake's shot had even singed his cloak. A second burst might do it.

But Jake didn't get the chance. Tepesch was on him now, lifting him up and tossing him away. Jake struck a pillar hard and didn't move.

Ben seized his own shock blaster. He had to help Lori. Tepesch was leaping toward her. With the Drac in him, he was invincible. Lori's aim seemed wayward, slow. Tepesch was moving at different speed. If only Ben could . . . but now Lori was in his way. Tepesch had hold of her and was using her as a shield. Ben couldn't fire for fear of hitting her.

Tepesch was yanking Lori's head back. Her hair streamed down like blond blood. The marks of her previous ordeal were still on her throat. Ben knew she couldn't recover from a second Drac attack.

"Lori!" Ben screamed. "Move! Move!"

She twisted in Tepesch's arms, and Ben's aim was true. The shot struck Vlad Tepesch, Prince of Wallachia, just below the collarbone. He let go of a choking Lori and gazed in disbelief at the hole in his chest. Lori and Ben gazed in disbelief, too. The shot should have paralyzed a man. Instead, it had opened Vlad up, revealing wires and gears and gleaming chips of metal worked in a travesty of life.

Ben fired a second time, a third, at the construct's unprotected body. Its innards shattered into fragments. Liquid flooded from its mouth. Not blood, but oil.

"I . . . I don't . . ." came the mechanical voice. "I . . . I don't . . ."

It clattered to the flagstones like scrap.

"I don't, either," gasped Ben. "Tepesch was a robot."

At that moment, thirty-five-thousand feet up and three-thousand miles away, the Vlad Tepesch, Prince of Wallachia, relaxed in the sumptuous splendor of his presidential jet with a small glass of something scarlet and sticky at his elbow.

"Come, Boris, your glumness is becoming tiresome," he said. "Enjoy the flight. We will soon be back in Wallachia."

"But, my prince . . ." Even Boris's whiskers seemed to droop with dismay.

"You think we have been defeated?" Tepesch permitted himself a wry chuckle. "You lack perspective, Boris. You lack patience. Perhaps, with the loss of the Cultural Exchange Building and its laboratories, we have suffered a minor setback. And perhaps, people now know a little more about us than I would like. But Drac production continues unabated elsewhere, does it not? And have we not also finally eliminated one of our main rivals for the drugs markets? Talon is dead, and his Serpent network scattered. We are stronger now than we were before, my loyal servant. Wallachia is stronger. Our day is coming. We have only to wait."

"But the children, my prince," Boris pursued, "those who escaped us, what of them?"

"Indeed." Vlad Tepesch seemed thoughtful. "Resourceful young people, were they not? Courageous and skillful, too. We underestimated them, Boris, and whichever secret organization they obviously belong to. Perhaps we should find out. One day, they might become formidable opponents. One day, perhaps, our paths will cross again."

"And then, my prince?"

"Oh, then, Boris, they will die."

They waited for Jake outside the cemetery gates. He needed time alone with Jennifer, and they respected that. Now that the excitement of the mission was over, her death had returned to haunt them.

"So how did we do?" Eddie wondered. "How did we really do? Plus or minus? Win or lose? Pride or shame?"

"I don't think missions can ever be as clear-cut as that," mused Lori. Ben's arm was around her, and she welcomed its comfort. "We just have to do the best we can and hope that that's enough."

"At least we struck a blow," said Cally thoughtfully, "a blow against drugs. The Serpents are out of operation, and the Wallachian building won't be producing anymore Drac. Every drug we stop from reaching the street gives someone a chance of a better life."

"That's good, Cal." Ben seemed to be encouraged by his teammates' words. "All right, so the real Vlad Tepesch escaped, but we hit the Wallachians where it hurt. And as for the Serpents, they're history. Talon's . . . well, we know about Talon. I think we've done a good job. I think we can hold our heads high. I think Mr. Deveraux is going to be pleased. That's got to be worth something, doesn't it?"

"Yeah, Ben," Eddie said with uncharacteristic gravity, "but Jennifer's life?"

Ben frowned and was silent.

"So what do we do about it?" pondered Cally.

"We learn," said Lori simply. "We move on. We remember her always, but we get on with our lives, our training. Risk is part of what we do — and sacrifice." She shrugged. "I don't know."

"One thing's for sure," Eddie observed, "when we get back to Spy High, things are never gonna be the same."

AN ENEMY WITHIN . . . ?

Turn the page for a sneak peek at

SPY HIGH:
MISSION FOUR

THE PARANOIA
PLOT

Available November 2004
Little, Brown and Company

An obstacle course had been set up in the extensive grounds to the rear of Deveraux Academy, with the operative word being "up." The obstacles, an assortment of poles, bars, hurdles, and hoops, hovered in the air about thirty meters above the ground. Corporal Keene controlled their height and position from a laptop. "It's designed to test your maneuverability," he was explaining. "Skybiking is not simply about speed. Now, who wants to play guinea pig?"

"I've always had a thing for little furry animals, Corporal Keene, sir," piped up Eddie, "and I'm a great mover."

"Very well, Nelligan," sighed Keene. "Let's see what you can do."

"Yes!" Eddie punched the air confidently. If there was one area of their training that he instinctively excelled at, it was skybiking. Vehicles were to Eddie what computers were to Cally. He grinned at their new teammate, tipped her a wink.

"Something in your eye, Ed?" Jake wondered.

Eddie ignored him, mounted his bike. At last, a chance to really impress her. He activated the magnetic engine and took to the skies. He'd be more than a match for any course set by Keene.

"Hey, what about some encouraging cheers?" he yelled down to his teammates. "Some light applause?"

"Get on with it, Nelligan!" snapped Keene. "We haven't got all day!"

"Thought you said it wasn't all about speed, sir," called Eddie, "but if time is pressing . . ."

He accelerated suddenly and startlingly, streaked toward the waiting obstacles.

If they were honest, Eddie's teammates and even Corporal Keene would have had to admit that he was pretty impressive.

At blurring speed, he zipped between poles and through loops, angled the SkyBike impeccably to negotiate the course, like a master skier tackling the Olympic slalom. His movements were fluid, liquid, human and machine in breathtaking harmony.

"Is this the same Eddie as yesterday or a different one?" Bond Team's new recruit asked Cally.

"There's only one Eddie," Cally said.

Who was arching now to make his return run. Maybe he shouldn't have waved just then. If he hadn't, maybe the others would have recognized the truth sooner. Though it probably wouldn't have made any difference if they had.

Eddie's SkyBike shot off so quickly he toppled backward and almost fell. "What's going on? What's he playing at?" Several people laughed. Eddie clowning about as always.

It happened suddenly as if the bike was alive and determined to throw its rider. It reared and plunged, veered dramatically from side to side. Eddie seemed to be holding on for dear life. It all looked more than faintly ludicrous.

"What do you think you're doing, Nelligan?" raged Keene. As the SkyBike charged drunkenly into the obstacles.

"I see what you mean, Cally. Same old Eddie. What a joker."

Cally, however, was not grinning. As Eddie ducked low to avoid one bar decapitating him. As a pole cracked painfully against his leg. "This isn't a joke," she realized. "I don't know how, but Eddie's in trouble." She looked for confirmation from the others. No laughter now. The danger was dawning on all of them. "His SkyBike's out of control."